DANGER, DANGER, EVERYWHERE!

"Lou   there?
Can yo

She   bumping of   rubber
pads or   against
the wo   have to
tell yo

Sudo   ring in
the air   g feeling—tl   o me,
please!   quiet.
"You're   nt on.
"There   nd. No
matter

Bantam Skylark Books of related interest
Ask your bookseller for the books you have missed

The Ghost Ferry

Emily Cates

A BANTAM SKYLARK BOOK

NEW YORK · TORONTO · LONDON · SYDNEY · AUCKLAND

Many thanks to Suzanne Weyn
for developing the original concept for
Haunting with Louisa

RL 4, 008–012

THE GHOST FERRY
A Bantam Skylark Book / March 1991

Bantam Books are published by Bantam Books, a division of Bantam Doubleday Dell Publishing Group, Inc. Its trademark, consisting of the words "Bantam Books" and the portrayal of a rooster, is Registered in U.S. Patent and Trademark Office and in other countries. Marca Registrada. Bantam Books, 666 Fifth Avenue, New York, New York 10103.

PRINTED IN THE UNITED STATES OF AMERICA
CWO   0 9 8 7 6 5 4 3 2 1

CHAPTER

1

Dee Forest stood on the wooden porch of Misty Island Inn. The warm ocean breeze ruffled her short, blond hair. She shut her eyes and lifted her face to the morning sun. Its rays made red and yellow patterns dance behind her lids. The leaves of the blackberry bushes that surrounded the porch rustled softly. The waves from the nearby ocean crashed against the rocky shore.

A car horn blared out on the road, and Dee's green eyes snapped open.

All through the frigid New England winter, she'd waited anxiously for summer to come to

Misty Island. But now that it was here, Dee wasn't so sure she liked it.

There were too many tourists. The streets and beaches teemed with them. The roads were clogged with cars and bikes. Suntanned vacationers whizzed around the island on rented mopeds. Dee was surprised to find that she resented their presence. These tourists seemed like intruders in a very private world.

She hadn't always felt so possessive of Misty Island. In fact, when she'd first arrived in the fall, it had seemed the most dismal, dreary place in the world. She had wanted to leave the second she'd stepped onto its long wooden ferry dock. The gray sky and chill winds had matched her mood perfectly.

Dee had come to live at her aunt Winnifred's Victorian inn several months after her mother had died in an automobile accident. That loss had been awful enough, but Dee sometimes felt that the drunken driver who'd killed her mother had taken her father's life as well. Though Mrs. Forest had been alone in the car, Dee's father was devastated by her death. At first he'd turned away from everything and everyone– including Dee–that reminded him of his wife.

Mr. Forest wanted to be strong for his daughter's sake, but his own grief was just too great.

Realizing that he wasn't coping well, he finally sent Dee off to stay with Aunt Win for the winter. And as she'd stood on the dock that bleak September day, she'd truly felt all alone in the world.

Dee had never been more miserable. But slowly—very slowly—wise and jolly Aunt Win had made her feel welcome and safe. Then, in the early spring, her father had joined her on the island and every day he seemed more himself. And for Dee, it was meeting Louisa that had roused her from her despair and self-pity.

Now Dee hummed softly under her breath as she began picking blackberries for breakfast. As she tossed them into a large plastic bowl, she couldn't resist popping a few of the warm, sweet berries into her mouth.

Two red-winged blackbirds soared past her. Nothing in the bleak winter months could have prepared her for the abundant beauty of summer on Misty Island.

Suddenly there was a stirring in the air. Dee put her bowl down on the ground. She cocked her head and listened. It was nothing she could hear—just a feeling. A presence.

"Louisa?" she whispered. "Is that you?"

There was no reply, just the soft song of the leaves around her. Yet the feeling persisted. "Louisa!" Dee called again.

Dee could feel the air grow warm around her. Then a pair of periwinkle-blue eyes framed by dark lashes floated in the air by her side. The rest of the ghostly figure soon followed. In another minute Dee was standing next to a delicate-boned girl her own age, thirteen. The girl wore a puff-sleeved white blouse under an ankle-length black pinafore. A tangle of auburn ringlets framed her pale oval face. She would have looked like a portrait from the turn of the century except for the bright pink high-topped sneakers peeking out from the hem of her dress.

"Louisa!" Dee cried. "I've been waiting for you."

"Sorry," said Louisa. "I still find materializing a bit tricky. It always takes me much longer than I expect it to."

Louisa Lockwood gracefully lifted her chin. Dee watched as her friend rose gently up into the air and effortlessly drifted over to the front

4

porch railing. Rising and floating was a difficult trick that always gave Louisa trouble. She kept practicing, though, determined to do it gracefully.

Louisa sat on top of the railing, letting her sneakers dangle over the side. "I'm getting rather good at this, don't you think?" she said, smiling proudly. "It's really just a matter of shifting one's weight. If I look up and inhale, I go up, and when I exhale and look down, I descend. Before I realized that, I was always rising and falling much too quickly. It simply takes practice."

"You are getting much better," Dee said. "What do you want to do today?"

"It's a beautiful morning, isn't it?" Louisa said quickly, looking uncomfortable, as if there were something she didn't want to talk about. Dee could see it in the way Louisa studied her graceful fingers instead of answering the question. Louisa was usually very direct.

"Yes, it's great," Dee replied. "Feel like going sailing on the bay?" Dee had taken sailing lessons the summer before, and all winter she'd looked forward to taking Louisa out and showing off her new skills.

Louisa held up a hand in front of her face. She closed her eyes and seemed to be concentrating very hard. In the next second her hand disappeared, though the rest of her stayed exactly where it was. Then her feet faded out. "Drat!" said Louisa, opening her eyes. "Every time I try to make my hand fade, my feet go away, too." As she spoke, her hand and feet reappeared.

"Why do you want to make your hand fade?" Dee asked.

"Because," Louisa said, giggling. "Because I can."

Dee realized that Louisa was still avoiding her question about their plans for the day. She didn't like the idea that Louisa wasn't being totally straight with her. In the months they'd known each other, they'd shared everything— their feelings, their dreams, even their clothing. Dee thought Louisa's high-button shoes looked great with her denim skirt, and Louisa felt very daring in Dee's sneakers.

Once Louisa materialized, Dee often forgot she was really a ghost. She seemed so much like any other girl—if she overlooked the old-fashioned clothing and a few outdated ideas.

Louisa was the real reason that Dee's winter on Misty Island had turned out to be so exciting. Even though she was a ghost, Louisa was the best friend Dee had ever had.

"Okay, Louisa, if you don't want to go sailing, what do you want to do?" Dee snapped.

"I apologize for not answering you right away," Louisa said. "I was just thinking, that . . . well . . . now that summer is here that you might want to . . . well . . ." Louisa's voice trailed off.

"Please say what's on your mind, Louisa," Dee said impatiently.

"I thought you might want to meet some girls and boys who aren't . . . aren't . . ." This time Louisa looked away sadly and then seemed to regain her nerve. "Who aren't dead!" she finished firmly.

The word "dead" echoed in Dee's ear. It seemed so strange when applied to Louisa. Dee's mother was dead, but not Louisa. How could a person who was dead walk and talk and be a friend? Yet Dee knew that Louisa *was* dead. She'd been killed in a fire back in 1897 along with her whole family.

"I don't want to hang out with anyone but

7

you," Dee answered firmly. "The island kids all stick together, and the tourists don't want to mix with the locals."

"I can't believe that's true of everyone," Louisa protested.

"Even if it isn't, they'd all seem boring next to you," Dee argued. Spending time with Louisa was certainly never boring. Ever since the night the ghost girl had first appeared in Dee's room, life had been one adventure after the other.

Being friends with a ghost had taken some getting used to. At first, Dee had feared that Louisa wanted to claim her body or kidnap her spirit or do any of the other strange things that TV ghosts were always doing.

But Louisa had assured her she simply wanted some company. She herself wasn't even sure what powers she had. After all, she'd been asleep for most of her ghostly existence. She'd only recently awakened at the very spot where her house had once stood. Of course, the inn was there now, built on the ashes of the old Lockwood home. And when Louisa saw how cozy Aunt Win had made Dee's room, so much like *her* old room, she'd decided to stay.

Dee was fascinated with her new friend and

wanted to know exactly how Louisa had come to this ghostly state. Louisa explained that after the fire she'd become separated from her family. For a while the ghost girl had despaired of finding her way into the next world. But then Louisa's mother came to her in a dream and told her that there *was* a way—she had only to help four of her living relatives.

It was clear from the beginning that Dee and Louisa had lots in common. But the thing that had cemented their friendship was the pursuit of Louisa's living relatives. Thrilled to have a project to throw herself into, Dee had dragged the naturally shy Louisa all over the island in search of her relatives. They'd had great success, too, quickly managing to help three relatives. But so far, they hadn't been able to find a fourth.

"I can't waste my time with other kids," Dee said now. "We still have to find another one of your relatives before you can rejoin your family."

Louisa sighed. "I'm not at all sure there are any more," she said. "It's a miracle that we've found three. The rest of my kin probably died or left the island a long time ago."

"You can't give up now," said Dee. "We're so close. Plus, I have an idea," she continued. "They're having a special exhibit at the Misty Island Museum this month. It's 'The People of Misty Island,' or something like that. Maybe we can pick up some clues there."

"I don't know," said Louisa. "I think I'd rather go sailing."

"Why didn't you say so in the first—" Dee broke off at the sound of the front screen door opening. Someone was coming.

A tall, heavyset woman with bright red hair stepped out onto the porch. "Who are you talking to, dear?" Aunt Win asked.

Dee's eyes darted up to the railing, and she breathed a sigh of relief. Louisa had disappeared.

CHAPTER
2

"Good morning, Aunt Win," Dee said with a smile.

"Good morning, dear," Winnifred Forest replied, giving Dee a hug and a kiss. "Did someone just leave?"

"That was me," Dee said, giggling nervously. "I was reciting a poem. Ummm . . . *The Rime of the Ancient Mariner.*" Dee spread her arms wide toward the ocean. "You know, 'Water, water, everywhere, but not a drop to drink,'" she recited dramatically.

Aunt Win chuckled. "There are certainly enough ancient mariners on this island. As a matter of fact, we're having one of them to dinner tonight."

"Jack Dodge?" Dee exclaimed happily. "That's the second time this week. I think he likes you, Aunt Win."

"That old coot!" Aunt Win laughed, looking pleased, nonetheless. "I've known him all my life. He is a cranky old dear. And he's bringing his grandson, Nicky."

Now it was Dee's turn to look pleased. Dee didn't like to admit it, even to herself, but Nicky Dodge interested her quite a lot. Although he'd never actually asked her out on a date, he did seem to like her. He was always very friendly when she ran into him on the beach or at his father's fish store where he worked on weekends. And he often seemed to look for excuses to visit the inn.

"Hurry with those blackberries," Aunt Win said, pushing the screen door open again. "I want to use them in my pancake batter."

"Let me get a few more and then I'll be right in," said Dee.

When the screen door creaked shut again, Louisa reappeared almost instantly. "Nicky Dodge is coming to dinner," she teased. "He's so handsome."

"He is cute," Dee agreed.

"Very," said Louisa with a wistful smile.

Dee knew that Nicky reminded Louisa of someone from her own past—a boy named Tobias Dodge who was undoubtedly related to Nicky. According to Louisa, the two looked very much alike.

"If we go sailing, you can wear my new tank suit," said Dee, changing the subject. "I want to wear my two-piece."

"You know I wouldn't," cried Louisa in a shocked voice.

"Oh, come on, just try it," Dee coaxed. "I bet it would look great on you. Besides, if you don't want anyone to see you, you can always disappear."

Louisa seemed to consider that for a moment, but then she shook her head. "No, I couldn't. I'd feel as if I were completely undressed. It wouldn't be proper."

"Nobody's proper anymore, Louisa," Dee argued. "That's one of the good things about being alive now."

Louisa pressed her lips together, all trace of laughter gone. "But I'm not alive now," she said flatly.

"Yes, you are, kind of," Dee insisted. "You're as good as alive."

Louisa shook her head. "No, I'm not. I don't feel the warmth of the sun, or smell the sea. I can't have a beau. I don't even know if I'll ever get any older. How will you feel when you're twenty. Will you still want to spend your time with a thirteen-year-old ghost girl?"

Dee didn't want to think about these things. "You're just changing the subject because you don't want to wear the bathing suit," she said.

Louisa shrugged, a gesture she'd learned from Dee. "Perhaps. All right—I agree to go sailing with you, but I most definitely refuse to wear that little slip of fabric you call a bathing suit. It isn't decent."

Dee couldn't help smiling. Some of Louisa's ideas seemed so odd to her.

"And don't laugh at me," Louisa said, smiling in spite of herself. "I know I often seem silly and old-fashioned to you. But that's the way I was raised. I can't change overnight."

Dee didn't have the heart to point out that almost a hundred years wasn't exactly overnight. She reached out to grab a very large berry off the bush. When she looked up she expected to see Louisa, but instead she found a pretty dark-haired woman looking down at her from the porch.

"Eva!" Dee gasped. Eva Barlow was a guest at the inn. She'd been there for so long—since early April—that she almost seemed like part of the family. Though Eva claimed she'd been working hard and needed a good long rest, Dee knew there was more to her extended stay than that. Dee's father and Eva had hit it off, and Eva was in no hurry to leave Misty Island. Her father clearly enjoyed Eva's company, but he insisted it was just a friendship—nothing more.

Eva laughed pleasantly. "I'm sorry. Did I startle you?"

"A little." Dee quickly looked around the porch. There was no sign of Louisa.

"They say you're getting old when you start talking to yourself," Eva said. "You'd better be careful."

Dee smiled nervously. "I know. I do that a lot."

"Your aunt asked me to tell you to come in. She needs help serving breakfast."

"Oh, no!" cried Dee. "I forgot she wanted these berries for her pancakes." She started up the steps.

"She must have gone ahead without them, because the guests are starting to eat," said Eva, following her inside.

Dee hurried into the wide dining room with its long pine table and antique china closet. "Sorry, Aunt Win," she apologized. "I lost track of the time."

"It's all right," said Aunt Win. "Just put the berries down in the kitchen and bring the tray of rolls out when you come back."

Dee did that and then helped with the rest of breakfast. The inn was completely filled with guests. They all looked tan and happy as they gulped down their delicious meal, eager to begin their day.

Of course Dee realized that Aunt Win ran an inn—and inns had to have guests. Still, she didn't like all these strangers milling around in her dining room, acting as if it were their own home. It felt like an invasion.

She couldn't wait to get out in the Sailfish. They'd sail out into the tranquil bay, away from all these noisy tourists. They were going to spend a wonderful morning, just she and Louisa.

CHAPTER

3

Dee quickly stacked the dishes inside the dishwasher. She was heading out the back door when her father entered the kitchen. He'd slept through breakfast and this was the first she'd seen of him that morning.

"Eva and I are taking windsurfing lessons over at the lake," Mr. Forest said as he hugged Dee. "Want to join us?"

"No thanks," Dee said brightly. "You and Eva don't need me along to get in your way."

Her father's blue eyes grew dark and serious. He ran an anxious hand through his hair. "You know you wouldn't be in the way, Dee. Besides, Eva and I are just friends."

"It's okay, Dad," Dee assured him. "I'm glad you've found such a nice girlfriend. Really." If her father was going to have a girlfriend, Dee couldn't think of a better one than Eva. Besides, he seemed a lot less sad since he'd met her.

"Dee, stop insisting that Eva's my girlfriend," he said. Then he laughed and shook his head. "I feel like a teenager, having this argument with you. We really are just friends, Eva and I."

"Okay, Dad," Dee said lightly. "If you say so."

As her father sat down at the kitchen table, Dee hesitated, then pushed open the screen door. "Well, so long," she said.

"Where are you going, honey?" he asked.

"Nowhere. Out."

Her father raised his eyebrows questioningly. "I'm going sailing over on Parker's Bay," Dee said.

"We'll go with you," said her father.

"You don't have to. I'm sure you'd rather windsurf."

Mr. Forest smiled. "Going with someone special? That nice Mason boy from school?"

18

"No, Dad," Dee said. "Jerry's up in Maine for the summer—with his grandparents. I'm going alone."

The serious look came back into her father's eyes. "Dee, you do almost everything alone. Aren't there some kids you'd like to be with? If you'd just go down to the beach, I'm sure you'd make lots of friends."

"Why does everyone want me to make new friends?" Dee said, thinking of the conversation she'd just had with Louisa.

"Has Aunt Win said something to you?" asked her father.

"No, not exactly," Dee replied. "I'm fine the way I am, Dad. Honest!"

Her father still looked doubtful. "Okay. Okay. I'll stop bugging you. Go ahead—and have a good time."

Dee pushed the door open and then ran back to plant a kiss on her father's cheek. "You don't have to worry about me, Daddy. Really," she said.

"All right, angel. I'll try not to worry," he said, forcing a smile. "Do you have money to rent a boat?"

"I have the twenty dollars you gave me last week."

"Don't forget to wear a life jacket," her father called as Dee bolted out the door. "I won't," she called back over her shoulder. Then, grabbing her old five-speed bike from the side of the inn, she whispered, "Okay, Louisa. Let's go."

There was a familiar stirring in the air as Louisa slowly came into view. She'd taken off her heavy pinafore and high-collar blouse. She wore a short-sleeved white petticoat that fell to her ankles. It was trimmed with blue ribbons and white eyelet lace. The bottom of the petticoat ruffled out with two layers of flounces. As usual, the pink high-tops peeked out from under the ruffles. "This is as daring as I'm going to get," she announced.

"You look great," Dee said admiringly.

"Since I don't have a summer frock, I decided to make do." Louisa looked down at her petticoat and blushed. "But I can't help expecting my grandmother to show up and start hollering at me for running around in my undergarments. She would think I'd gone completely mad."

"You look great!" Dee repeated. "I wish we

wore such pretty underthings. Your hair looks neat that way, too." Louisa had caught her dark red curls up in a ponytail and tied it with a blue satin ribbon.

"Thank you," Louisa said shyly. "I always wear it up in summer."

Dee swung her leg over the bar of her boy's-style bike. "It seems a waste for you to ride on the bike with me, when you can just sort of fly beside me," she said.

"But I want to do it," Louisa said eagerly. "I've never ridden on a bicycle. Old Mr. Tibbits used to have a big three-wheeler, but I've never been on one like this."

"Okay, sit here," said Dee.

Cautiously, Louisa settled herself on the handlebars. "Ready," she said.

Dee pushed off on her bike, amazed to find that Louisa was light as a feather. Except for the fact that she had to look over Louisa's shoulder to steer, it was as if no one was there at all.

Wobbling down the long gravel drive, they came out onto the curving road that wrapped around Misty Island. To their right, the land dipped sharply down in a rocky slope that ended at the water. They looked along the shore and saw two figures fishing on the jetty that stretched deep into the sea. Farther up was a sandy beach already dotted with the summer swimmers' colorful umbrellas and swimsuits. Large fluffy clouds rolled lazily across the blue sky above them.

The pair headed toward town, Dee breathing heavily as she pedaled up the steep road. They passed a low brick church and, on the other side, a sprawling white hotel called the May House, which had been boarded up all winter. Now a steady stream of cars drove up and down its blacktopped drive, and the huge front lawn was filled with guests, some playing badminton, others sunning themselves on white lawn chairs.

Dee wiped the perspiration from her brow when they reached the top of the hill. The worst was over. Soon they were zooming downhill, Dee with her feet stuck out from either side of the bike.

"This is so exciting," Louisa cried gleefully, making no attempts to brush back the strands of hair blowing around her face.

They whizzed past several guest houses and

two craft shops before Dee pressed the hand-brakes to stop at the one and only traffic light on Misty Island. Louisa was smiling radiantly. "Oh, that was fun!" she breathed.

"You weren't scared?" Dee asked, glad to see Louisa so happy.

"I was scared," Louisa admitted. "Deliciously frightened. But then I just reminded myself that I have no cause for fear. I'm a ghost! Nothing can hurt me."

"Well, the road is flatter from here on," Dee assured her.

"I think I'd best disappear now," said Louisa. "I wouldn't want anyone in town to see me in this garment."

"They'd just think you looked cute," said Dee. "Take a chance."

Louisa's eyes shone with mischief. "I'll do it. But what if someone you know sees us and asks who your friend is?"

"I'll say you're a tourist, that's all."

"All right, let's go."

The main street through town was already jammed with cars, bicycles, mopeds, and tour-ists on foot. Dee maneuvered her bike through the crowd, past more craft shops, gift shops, restaurants, and souvenir stands. Only the fish market, the general store, and the old Misty Island Cafe and Clam Bar were familiar to them. Those were open all winter. The other shops were closed until summer. It was as if the town had been hibernating all winter and had suddenly awakened.

The ten o'clock ferry had apparently just docked. People loaded down with suitcases and backpacks flooded the street. "Look, Mom, that's the dress I want," they heard one teenage girl say. She was pointing at Louisa.

It took only five minutes to reach the other side of town. Here the shops and inns were somewhat farther apart. Dee braked at a stop sign in front of a quaint little gift shop. To her right, the road led off to the best beaches, Parker's Bay and Loon Lake at the tip of the crescent-shaped island. To her left was the Misty Island Museum.

Dee headed off to the right, where the road skirted the ocean and was very level. Dee pedaled quickly. As she did Louisa turned to her. "Watch this," she said.

Without a moment's hesitation, Louisa stood straight up on the handlebars and spread her arms wide. "I'm a sail, blowing in the breeze," she shouted.

"Hey, I can't see with your skirt blowing in my face!" Dee laughed, pushing away the billowing petticoat.

Louisa pulled her skirt up to her knees. "Louisa! I'm shocked!" teased Dee.

"I don't care!" cried Louisa. "It's a beautiful day and I'm riding on a bicycle in my petticoat."

Dee could see that the summer day had brought out Louisa's more adventurous instincts. She gasped with delight when Louisa rose into the air, her dress fluttering like the wings of a great white bird. Louisa slowly drifted to the back of the bike, then grabbed onto the seat and let Dee pull her along.

"Louisa, someone will see you," Dee cried as an old gray pickup came chugging up the road. She realized she and Louisa had suddenly switched roles. Now *she* was the one who was worried about what people would think.

"You're right," said Louisa. And with that, she pulled herself up onto the bike seat behind Dee.

"I wish I could do those things," said Dee, glancing back toward Louisa as they rode along.

Though her eyes were still bright, the smile quickly faded from Louisa's lips. "No, you don't," she said. "If you could do those things you'd be a ghost."

"Maybe I'd like that!" Dee exclaimed.

"I don't think so," said Louisa.

CHAPTER

4

Dee dropped the bike at a sand dune and headed down toward Parker's Bay. Still visible, Louisa took off the pink sneakers and walked barefoot on the soft sand. Dee kicked off her sneakers to do the same. "Ouch," she said, "the sand's hot already."

"I can't feel it," said Louisa, blithely walking along.

"That's another good thing about being a ghost," Dee said.

"No," Louisa disagreed. "It's better to feel things."

By the shore was a row of sailboats for rent.

A husky blond man in blue swimming trunks sat on a beach chair beside them. Dee requested one of the small, two-person Sailfish. "You know how to use it?" the man asked.

"I got my Red Cross certificate last summer," Dee announced proudly.

"If you're good enough for the Red Cross, you're good enough for me," he said. "And your friend, here, can she swim?"

"Dee saw that Louisa was about to shake her head no. "Like a fish," Dee told him.

The man laughed. "Okay, be sure you wear these anyway," he said, holding out two orange life jackets. He waited till they put them on, then handed Dee the boat's tiller, rudder, and centerboard.

"You're the kid from the Misty Island Inn aren't you?" he asked, dragging the hull of the fiberglass boat into the water.

"That's right," Dee said as she threw the shorts and shirt she'd worn over her suit onto the sand. She looked at the man. She had no idea who he was. Thinking fast, she said, "I didn't recognize you without your beard." A lot of the local men wore full, bushy beards in winter and then shaved them off in summer.

"Yeah, it's too hot to wear now," the man said, rubbing his chin. "No charge for the boat today. We islanders have to stick together."

"Thanks," Dee said.

He put the sail into the boat and helped Dee attach the rudder. "She's all yours," he said. Then, turning to Louisa, he said, "You going to sail in that pretty dress?"

"Uh . . . I burn easily," she answered shyly.

"Be careful then," he said, returning to his rental boats.

The girls pulled the boat out farther. Then Dee scrambled on, placed the centerboard in the slot, and hoisted the red-and-yellow-striped sail. Dee put out her hand to help her friend, but Louisa just hopped aboard without any effort at all.

Before long, Dee was cutting a zigzag path, tacking upwind.

"This is so thrilling," said Louisa. "I lived on this island for thirteen years and never actually went on a boat. And what a beautiful boat," she added, running her delicate hand along the shiny red fiberglass. "All our boats were made of wood. This is so smooth."

Dee just nodded happily. Sometimes seeing

things through Louisa's eyes was like seeing them for the very first time.

Louisa pulled off her blue ribbon and let her hair blow free in the breeze. Dee had often thought that even if Louisa were a live modern girl, there would be something especially lovely and otherworldly about her. She'd never felt it more so than at this moment.

The girls didn't speak as the boat skimmed across the waves. Dee let her mind wander. She wondered what would happen when the summer was over. Would she and her father stay on the island or return to Cambridge? She was a little surprised to realize that she was hoping they'd stay. She hadn't liked the island or its inhabitants at first, but now she was starting to change her mind. "I feel bad that I didn't recognize the boat rental man," said Dee, breaking the silence. "How do you suppose he knows me?"

"He's the man who tends those tanks behind the inn," said Louisa dreamily, as if Dee had roused her from some serious thoughts of her own. "What do they call them, for the inside hot water?"

"Propane tanks."

"That's right."

"I never really noticed him," Dee said.

"Maybe you should start paying more attention to the people around you," said Louisa, gazing across the bay.

"Don't start that again, please," said Dee.

The bay looked like a large lake except for the narrow channel that led out to the sea. It was a popular place to sail because it wasn't as choppy as the ocean, yet the ocean breeze blew through.

Today the bay was filled with small sailboats. "We never had colored sails like this," Louisa noted. "It's so pretty. They look like giant butterflies skimming the surface of the water. The sails flutter and flap like wings."

The girls sailed for almost an hour, until they reached the mouth of the channel, and then they decided to head back. "This is going to be perfect," said Dee. "The wind is behind us. We'll practically fly back."

"Prepare to come about!" she called out, using the term she'd learned in sailing class to warn all crew members to stay low. She pushed the tiller away from her and made a quick turn.

The boom of the sail swung across as the boat quickly turned.

Instantly the sail filled with wind and they picked up speed, cutting through the water at a sharp angle. "Lean back," Dee yelled, gripping the sail's line. The sail side of the boat was tipping down toward the water. They'd have to balance their weight against the opposite side to keep it from going over.

"Hold on to the sides," Dee said, laughing at the sight of Louisa's wide-eyed amazement.

The boat sped back toward shore. "Want to tip it?" asked Dee.

"What?" cried Louisa, aghast at the suggestion.

"If I pull in the sail, we can go faster and faster, until the boat tips over."

"Isn't that dangerous?" asked Louisa.

"No. You just jump on the centerboard under the boat and it comes right up," Dee answered. "What do you say?"

"All right!" Louisa shouted. "I feel reckless today."

Dee tugged on the line and pulled the sail in tight. The boat tilted at an even sharper angle. "Oh, my goodness!" cried Louisa. And then, suddenly, they were flying over backward as the boat flipped in the opposite direction.

"You okay?" Dee asked, coming up to the surface and suddenly remembering Louisa had said she couldn't swim.

"Yes," Louisa called beside her in the water. "I can't swim, but I just realized I don't need to. If I can float in the air, I can surely float in the water. Besides, I'm wearing this," she added, pointing to the orange vest.

Dee swam quickly to the side of the boat and grabbed hold of the centerboard jutting out from its bottom. She pulled down on the board, but the boat didn't right itself as she'd expected. She climbed up higher on the side of the boat and pulled down as hard as she could.

"What's the matter?" Louisa called from the other side.

"I think I let the sail get too wet. There's a lot of water in it," Dee called back, trying not to panic.

Just then two little boats headed toward them from the middle of the bay, one with a yellow sail, one with a blue. "Need some help?" called a teenage girl on the first boat to arrive—the yellow one. Without waiting for an answer, the

33

other girl jumped into the water and swam to the tip of the overturned sail.

"Better get this up fast or it'll turn turtle on you," she called. "Once it's upside down, you can forget it."

The blue boat arrived with another teenage girl and a boy. The boy sized up the situation and jumped in. Together with the girl already in the water, he helped push the sail up as Dee pressed on the centerboard. It only took minutes to right the boat.

"Thanks a million," Dee said, hanging on to the side of the boat.

"No problem," said the boy, climbing back onto his boat.

"You on vacation?" the first girl on the other boat asked.

"I live here," Dee said proudly.

"Neat," said the girl who'd helped with the sail. "We're all staying at The Seagull Inn. I'm Jessie, and that's Karen, Ken, and Julie. Why don't you come back with us? They're throwing a barbecue at the inn."

"Sorry, I can't," Dee said. "But thanks for your help, too."

"Okay. If you change your mind, we'll be there," said the girl named Julie.

As the two boats sailed off, Dee climbed back into the Sailfish. "Louisa?" she called, looking down into the water. She turned around and was startled to find Louisa standing right next to her. "Where did you disappear to?"

"I wanted to give you a chance to make friends," she said. "I wish you'd said yes to that barbecue tonight."

"I didn't think you'd find it fun," Dee said, surprised.

"I wouldn't be going—you would," Louisa argued.

"I couldn't leave you alone," Dee insisted. "Not ever."

CHAPTER

5

On the way back from Parker's Bay, Louisa was unusually quiet. No trace of her carefree mood remained. She sat on the handlebars of Dee's bike, but she didn't speak or do any stunts. She seemed deep in thought.

When they came to the fork in the road near the Misty Island Museum, Dee noticed the banner over its door for the first time. It said: "Misty Island—The People and Places."

"Hey," said Dee, "that's the exhibit I told you about. Let's take a look."

Louisa hopped off the handlebars. She gazed

at the museum and then back at Dee. There was a look of great anxiety on her face. "I'm not sure I'm ready," she said.

"All right. I just thought maybe we could get a clue to where your fourth relative might be," said Dee.

Louisa looked back at the museum. She breathed deeply and squared her shoulders. "You're right. There might be some helpful information in there. I think we should go."

"Are you sure?" Dee checked. Louisa nodded. "Then why don't you just disappear until we get inside," Dee suggested. "They charge a dollar at the door."

"A very good idea," said Louisa with a small smile. She stepped behind a thick pine—and didn't appear to step back out. A gentle tap on Dee's shoulder told her that Louisa was now invisible and right by her side.

They headed across the street toward the museum. It was certainly nothing like any of the grand showcases Dee had visited when she'd gone into Boston with her mother and father. This was a small white house with green shutters and an open porch that stood on a wide, flat plot of land.

Dee walked her bike up the flagstone path and leaned it against the porch. She climbed the steps and paid her dollar to the small elderly woman in plaid shorts and a yellow shirt who sat at the entrance table.

As soon as she entered the cool, dark house, Dee knew there would be no statues or great works of art. This museum was devoted to the history of Misty Island. One room showed the fishing boats and equipment the early settlers had used. Another displayed the dresses the settler women had sewed themselves. A third room was full of spinning wheels and looms.

"Have you ever been here before?" Dee whispered to the invisible Louisa.

"No, I haven't," Louisa answered in a small, awed voice. "Who would imagine all of these everyday items would someday be considered unusual?"

Dee had been there once before and thought it was all pretty dull. She knew there was more to the island's history than spinning wheels and fish hooks. She'd heard stories of settlers and Indians doing battle on the high bluffs at the south side of the island in the 1600s. And after that, there were tales of pirates and shipwrecks.

According to legend, some people actually lured ships near Misty Island's rocky coast at night by holding lit lanterns on the cliffs, giving the impression that the coast was safe. When the ships crashed against the rocks, they'd wade out into the waters and loot them. Though the current islanders denied the story, Dee thought it might be true.

These were the kinds of things that interested her, not hundred-year-old oxen yokes. That's why her eyes went wide with interest as she looked over this new exhibit. For one thing, it was about people. Sepia-toned portraits lined the walls, many of them men with full, bushy beards and serious expressions. The women wore their hair tied back and turned their stern, weather-lined faces toward the photographer. The people of Misty Island stood in family groups in front of modest wooden homes or posed proudly by their fishing boats.

One wall featured a handsome bearded man holding a pick ax. Framed beside his picture were several letters written from California. He'd gone there to follow the gold rush in 1849 and later returned to become mayor of Misty Island. Dee noticed that his name was Nicholas

Dodge. Next to him was a picture of another man in a baggy World War One uniform. It was captioned Tobias Dodge.

"Is that him?" Dee whispered.

She heard a small gasp of astonishment beside her. "It is. It is Tobias. All grown up and handsome," said Louisa sadly. Dee knew Louisa'd had a crush on him, but she had no idea how he had felt about Louisa. Would he have married her if she'd lived?

The letters framed next to Tobias Dodge's picture were addressed to his father. They spoke of how lonely and war-weary he was, and how he longed to return to Misty Island. A note at the bottom reported that he had indeed come home, following in his father's footsteps as mayor.

Stepping closer to the picture, Dee studied the lively eyes that peered out from under his helmet. She was amazed at how much he resembled Nicky Dodge. There was no doubt about it—they were clearly related.

Dee moved on to another wall, which featured an enlarged photograph of an old-fashioned ferry. Women in twenties-style dress and men in white summer pants and jackets were boarding the boat. "Look at this, Louisa," Dee said, moving closer to examine the writing next to the photo. "It says this is the famous ghost ferry." She read the small script. "Before it left on its fateful journey—"

Dee cut herself short. She thought she heard a stifled gasp and then a soft snuffling sound. Was Louisa crying? "Are you okay, Louisa?" Dee asked quietly. "Is this exhibit too painful for you?"

"It's—it's—" Louisa began in a choked voice. "It's just that so much has happened since I died. I never even saw that ferry. I never saw Tobias grow to manhood. I . . ." Louisa's voice trailed away.

"We shouldn't have come here. We can go," Dee said. "I didn't mean to upset you, Louisa."

"No, no, you stay," Louisa's teary voice insisted. "I have to go."

"Wait, I'll come with you," said Dee. But Louisa didn't answer. Dee assumed she'd fled the building. She ran toward the door, eager to comfort her.

She was in such a hurry to get out the door that she didn't see Mrs. Lockwood until she'd almost walked right into her. "Ohhh! Sorry,

Mrs. Lockwood," Dee said, jumping back awkwardly.

A tiny woman with wavy brown hair and dark lively eyes, Mrs. Lockwood put out a delicate hand to steady Dee. "Hello, dear," she said. "Interesting exhibit, isn't it?"

"Yes, very interesting," Dee agreed quickly. She wanted to get past, but Mrs. Lockwood was standing right in the middle of the doorway.

"I wish someone had told me about it sooner, though," she continued. "As you know, I have albums and albums of old photos, collecting dust in my attic. I would have liked to see my family represented in this collection."

Dee nodded. She'd have liked that, too, since Mrs. Lockwood was one of Louisa's relatives they'd already managed to locate and help out. They'd seen some of her albums but not all of them.

"Would it be all right if I came over and had another look at them sometime?" Dee asked politely.

"Certainly, dear," said Mrs. Lockwood. "Come anytime. Anytime at all."

"Thanks," said Dee. "Excuse me now, but I have to go catch up with a friend."

"Run right along, dear, and say hello to your aunt for me," Mrs. Lockwood said as Dee ran out onto the porch.

"Louisa?" Dee whispered. But there was no reply.

A moment later Mrs. Lockwood came back out to the porch. "I just had a thought, Dee. If you're interested in this sort of thing, you might want to look around the graveyard. It's quite fascinating. Have you been there?"

"Once," Dee answered, "and just for a minute. Maybe I should check it out again."

"Yes, but I wouldn't go now," Mrs. Lockwood said. "It looks like rain," she added before stepping back into the museum.

Dee realized that Mrs. Lockwood was right—in the short time she'd been inside the museum, the sunny day had turned ominous. Giant thunderclouds loomed black in the sky, and a chilly wind whipped the flag outside the museum. She lifted her hand. The air felt moist but no drops were falling yet.

It occurred to Dee that one way to cheer Louisa up would be to find some clue to her fourth relative's whereabouts. Although she'd known the graveyard would be a good place to look for clues, she had purposely avoided it. Louisa's grave was there, and Dee found it too unnerving to think of her friend in that way.

But now Dee checked the sky and decided to chance a visit to the graveyard. She was determined to find a relative for Louisa to help. Glancing at the sky one more time, she hopped on her bike and pedaled toward the cemetery.

CHAPTER

6

Dee coasted around the S-shaped curve and stopped short at the bottom of the hill. Leaving the bike by the rickety fence that surrounded the sloping graveyard, she picked her way among the worn, chipped granite stones. She was reminded of the people in the old photos in the museum. Once, long ago, they'd been just as alive as she was right now.

The mournful blast of the lighthouse horn made her jump. She could feel the dampness on her clothing, see the eerie clouds of mist rolling low to the ground.

She bent and read the gravestone closest to her. DESIRE HODGES, 1739–1759. She continued to read the epitaph under Desire's name.

As you pass by, cast an eye.
As you are now, so once was I.
As I am now, so must you be.
Prepare for death and follow me.

A cold chill ran up Dee's back. The foghorn sounded again. Dee pushed her damp hair up off her forehead and tried to think logically. On her last visit to this spot, she'd noticed that there'd only been about fifteen families on Misty Island in the 1800s. Their surnames repeated on the gravestones over and over. By reading carefully, one could tell how the families had intermarried, could follow a family's history through many generations. Around 1920, new names began to show up on the stones as people from the mainland began moving to the island. From then on, it was harder to keep track of the families.

Dee knew Louisa's family was located farther up the hill. She began the climb.

The oldest stones were at the bottom of the

hill. They dated back to the 1700s. As Dee got to the 1800s, the stones in that section became more ornate. Praying hands, ivy wreaths, cherubs, and doves were carved into the granite. Some stones obviously marked the graves of sailors. They were decorated with anchors.

Dee stopped to examine the stone of a Captain Ackurs Paine. There were two smaller stones on the right and two on the left. Dee looked at them, too. They were the four wives of Ackurs Paine. The captain had outlived them all.

Dee stopped again when the name Lockwood started to appear on the stones. That was Louisa's family. With a quick shudder, she looked past the smooth marble stone with the name LOUISA carved in an arch across the top. Beside that stone were her mother, father, and younger brother. There were other Lockwoods nearby. Dee began reading the names. "Melanie Agnes Lockwood Paine," she read, "beloved daughter of Icivilla and Jason Lockwood and loving wife of Ezra Paine."

She looked back at Captain Paine's grave. Ezra might have been his son. She'd have to go back and see if there was a grave for the child of Ezra and Melanie Paine.

Dee sighed. This was going to be a lot of work. Maybe it would be better to save it for a sunny day.

Suddenly Dee was startled by a rustling sound just behind her. She was sure no one else had been nearby a moment ago. She turned around nervously, then looked to both sides. No one was there. She exhaled slowly to calm herself. It was probably just a rabbit.

But there it was again. Dee turned around again, and this time she gasped at the sight before her. A few feet away the orange tiger lilies that grew wild on the island and throughout the graveyard began to rise, one by one, up out of the ground.

Dee clasped her hand over her mouth and watched, wide-eyed, as each flower rose up to join the others, which were hovering together in the air. Then, all together, they floated over to the grave of Louisa's mother. A bunch of flowers rained down there, and a few more settled onto her father's and her brother's graves. There were still about five more flowers floating above the graves.

Dee relaxed. "Louisa?" she called. The remaining flowers dropped to the ground. Slowly Louisa appeared.

"You startled me," she said, gathering up the flowers at her feet.

"I startled *you?*" Dee giggled in relief. "You almost gave me a heart attack."

"Sorry. I guess I was lost in my own thoughts," Louisa answered. "Besides, you look like a ghost yourself, standing there so still with the fog boiling up all around you."

"I'm sorry I dragged you to the museum," said Dee. "It must have been horrible seeing all the people you once knew and knowing that they're all . . . all gone now."

"I don't know how to describe the feeling. It was so overwhelming," Louisa said softly. "It seems just months ago that I was talking to some of those people. It's all so real to me. But, as you say, it's all gone—*long* gone!"

"Don't think about it," said Dee, wishing she could do something, anything, about Louisa's sadness.

"I *have* to think about it, Dee. I had to come here to make it real. I'll tell you something, though. In some strange way, it cheered me up to come here."

"I don't understand," Dee said, giving Louisa a worried look.

Louisa smiled faintly and there was a faraway look in her eyes. "I was remembering that they used to call this Cotton Hill," she said, her eyes lighting up at the thought.

Dee looked around. There wasn't a cotton plant anywhere. It was much too cold to grow cotton on Misty Island.

"I remember the day of my thirteenth birthday," Louisa went on. "There was a terrible storm. Papa boarded up the windows, along with everyone else in town. A big, two-masted schooner was caught in the storm. We could see it from the shore, pitching and tossing. Some of the men tried to go to its aid, but it was no use. Their boats just got beaten back by the waves. Old Mr. Sands almost died himself. We all stood down on the dock in our rain gear watching that poor ship until long after nightfall."

"How awful," said Dee. "Awful, but exciting."

"It was awful for those poor men on the

ship," said Louisa seriously. "By the morning the storm was over, but there was no sign of the ship. It was completely destroyed. The men went out and recovered the bodies. They brought them back and buried them right here."

"Did anyone survive?" Dee asked.

Louisa shook her head. "No. But folks used to say the spirits roamed this island as ghosts. Though, now that I'm a ghost, I can tell you I've never seen a one of them. I'm quite sure that I'm the only ghost on Misty Island."

"What does that have to do with Cotton Hill?" asked Dee.

"Well, sad as all that was, some good came out of it, for us islanders, anyway. It turned out that the ship was carrying a cargo of cotton—bolts and bolts of it. In the next few days it all floated ashore, along with the wreckage from the ship. Cotton wasn't easy to come by then, and the women were most excited. They tied their skirts around their knees and waded right out into the surf to gather it up. I remember, it got to be like a holiday. They even let us out of school to go help carry in the cotton."

Louisa folded her arms and looked down the

hill. "In those days the graveyard didn't come up so far," she said. "We carried the cotton up this hill and spread it out in the sun to dry. It was all waterlogged and weighed near a ton, but you should have seen it, Dee. It was beautiful. There were calico prints, and purple paisleys from India. There was even a bolt that was as red-orange as the sunset. The minister's wife said it was too brazen, and later she dyed it black, but on that day you could see it sitting up here on the hill for miles."

"It must have looked beautiful," said Dee, imagining the colorful fabric fluttering in the sunlight.

"It did." Louisa smiled happily. "And I remember struggling up the hill with one heavy bolt and suddenly the weight became as light as a feather. I turned and there was Tobias Dodge. He'd come along and picked up the back end. It seems like yesterday. I remember how the sun felt on my face and how the flowers looked like specks of gold poking up among the material. I remember how it felt when Tobias touched my hand as we spread the material on the ground."

Louisa lowered her eyes modestly, clearly

embarrassed by the memory. Then she looked at the tiger lilies in her hands. "I was going to put these last flowers on his grave up the hill."

"Put the flowers there, and then let's go home," said Dee. "I came to find a relative for you, but I can do that tomorrow."

"I'm not going back with you," Louisa said firmly.

"Why not?" Dee demanded.

Louisa bent and began untying the pink sneakers. "Because I've made a decision," she said without looking up. She took off the shoes and held them out to Dee. "Here, take these back."

"Louisa, the ground is wet. Put those back on," Dee said.

"Don't you see?" Louisa exploded. "I keep telling you! It doesn't matter to me if the ground is wet, or cold, or covered with snow. It doesn't matter if the sand is hot, or if I fall off a sailboat. I'm a ghost! I'm already dead!"

"Yes, but—" Dee began.

"And you're alive. You should be spending your time with people who are also alive, like those young folks back at the bay. You're too much alone, and it's my fault. I've distracted you from making friends. I want you to go to that barbecue tonight. You've got to go."

"But, Louisa, I don't—"

"I thought I could stand seeing the pictures of the people I once knew," Louisa continued. "But I couldn't. It made me very, very sad. And the photographs made me realize . . ." Louisa's blue eyes filled with tears, which she wiped away quickly. "I realized that truly I'm dead. Of course, I've always known it in my head, but spending this winter with you has made it seem unreal. Today I almost fooled myself into thinking I was alive again. But I'm not. The photographs made that very clear."

"I don't mind that you're a ghost," said Dee.

"But it's not fair to you. You're a live girl. I'm turning *you* into a ghost, too, Dee! Look at yourself! Lurking around graveyards in the fog! I've been very selfish—and very unfair to you."

"But I *want* to spend time with you, Louisa," Dee insisted helplessly.

Louisa looked away. When she looked back, her expression had changed. Her delicate chin was set firmly and her eyes were narrowed.

"Perhaps I don't wish to spend all my time with you!" she said.

"Why not?" Dee wailed. "What have I done?"

"Oh, nothing," Louisa said tenderly, back to her old self. But then, in a flash, she was angry again. "I mean nothing interesting. I'm a ghost. I can fly. I can become invisible and pass through solid objects. Don't you think I'd rather do those things than *hang around* with a . . . mortal?"

Dee was dumbstruck. It hadn't occurred to her that Louisa might feel this way. And she wasn't totally convinced that she did.

"I've finally gotten it into my head that I'm a ghost, and ghosts have special powers. I'm going to enjoy them," Louisa finished. "You're getting too boring."

That last shot made Dee angry. "Boring?" she cried. "Boring!" How could she argue, though? If Louisa found her boring, how could she defend herself? "You're the one who's boring!" she yelled back, looking for something equally hurtful to say. "All you want to do is return to your past. Well, go ahead. I can manage very well without you!"

55

Louisa recoiled from Dee's harsh words.

"If you think I'm so boring," she said, "maybe I should just leave now."

"I only said that because you said—" Dee began, but Louisa was already gone. "Don't you dare dematerialize in the middle of a fight!" Dee shouted. "Come back here!"

Louisa didn't answer. Dee waited. Not a sound. She stood, hands on hips, looking around the foggy graveyard. She was all alone. She could feel it. Louisa was gone.

All that remained were the bright pink high-tops sitting on the cold, hard ground.

CHAPTER
7

She'll get over it, Dee thought hopefully as she pushed some peas around on her plate. *Louisa is entitled to her moods just like anyone else.*

Winnifred Forest served her guests one meal a day—breakfast. After that, they were on their own. Dinner was just for family and, sometimes, friends. Tonight Aunt Win had prepared a particularly delicious dinner: roast lamb, mint peas, and her own creamy, rich mashed potatoes.

Normally Dee would have been in heaven, but tonight she had no appetite. She was still too upset over her argument with Louisa.

She looked across the table at Nicky Dodge, who was eating heartily. He hadn't said much all night, but his bright blue eyes shone with interest at the conversation going on around him. His grandfather and Aunt Win were trading gossip about the local townspeople.

Dee could see that old Jack, with his deeply lined face, intense blue eyes, and full head of snowy white hair, bore a strong resemblance to the Dodge family pictures at the museum. She figured he must be about seventy now. That meant he would have been just a small child when Louisa's Tobias was a young man.

Now he was just finishing his account of the fishing trip he and Nicky had taken that afternoon. " . . . and so young Nick and I are heading in while Lavinia Cottsworth is standing on the shore screaming at us to pull in farther down," he said gruffly. "Says we're disturbing the lobster traps."

"Oh, that Lavinia thinks she just owns the whole island," Aunt Win agreed as she cut more lamb.

"Any fool knows that the lobster traps are out farther," Jack grumbled. "I'll grant you that something's gone dead wrong with those traps.

They haven't had a catch in two weeks. The guys are near tearing their hair out."

"We're just about out of lobster down at the store," Nicky chimed in. "Dad says we're going to have to start buying them off-island if this keeps up."

"But how on earth Lavinia gets around to blaming us for the darned traps being off, I'll never know," Jack grumbled. "That woman has cobwebs where her brains ought to be."

"Isn't she the mayor's wife?" asked Dee's father, who was sitting between Dee and Eva.

"Isn't she ever!" Aunt Win exclaimed. "She'd have the words 'Mayor's Wife' tattooed on her forehead if she thought she could get away with it."

"She does seem proper," said Eva, tucking a piece of her blunt-cut brown hair behind her ears. Dee noticed that she was already getting tan. The new color made her look younger and very pretty.

"She may be prim and proper now," Jack scoffed, "but I remember one time when Lavinia drank too much of Grandpa Small's hard cider and stood up on a table, singing that crazy song . . . what was it, Winnie?"

Aunt Win burst out laughing. "I remember it. I remember—" She had to catch her breath before she could go on. "It was called, 'Never Throw a Lighted Lamp at Mother!' "

Jack Dodge pounded the table with his gnarled, old hands. "That was it! That was it!" he wheezed.

"And Fred Cottsworth almost called off the wedding," Aunt Win picked up the story. "Oh, that was a long, long time ago indeed."

Nicky caught Dee's eye. His shoulders were shaking with laughter. Dee responded with a weak smile. She was glad to see him, but her thoughts were elsewhere. She couldn't bring herself to join in the fun. It was as though she were being bombarded with the past today. The history of Misty Island was becoming so vivid in her mind. So much life had been lived on this island. How could it all just disappear without a trace?

As soon as the dishes were cleared, the party moved out onto the porch. Everyone grabbed sweaters and jackets since the fog was still heavy. Despite the dampness, the cool air felt refreshing after the heavy dinner.

Aunt Win set scented candles in glass jars

along the porch railing to keep the bugs away. The only other light was a yellow bulb over the front door. The lamp that usually illuminated the front sign had burned out the night before.

Aunt Win passed around a tray of coffee and hot cider, and everyone settled down to drink. The adults took the wicker chairs. Nicky planted himself on the railing, and Dee sat on the porch floor with her back against a post.

Dee glanced up at Nicky and he smiled at her. *What a nice smile he has*, Dee thought. She wanted him to like her, but tonight she just couldn't get her mind off Louisa.

The fog was so thick that the lapping of the waves was the only proof that the ocean hadn't disappeared altogether. The dull blast of the lighthouse foghorn now sounded every ten minutes. Dee looked at the faces around her. It was amazing how the jumping shadows cast by the flickering candles made even kindly Aunt Win's face seem frightening.

Suddenly Jack Dodge jumped out of his seat and pointed out to the ocean. "There it is! Well, what do you know!"

Eva stood and leaned against the rail. "There's

what?" she asked, peering out into the dark night.

"The light. Didn't you see it?"

"I didn't see anything," said Eva.

"Nobody else saw it?" asked Jack. The others shook their heads. "I'm sure it was there—just for a second," the old man said, sitting back down.

"What did you see?" Nicky asked.

"The lights of the ghost ferry," Jack said matter-of-factly. He took a sip of his coffee and sat forward before going on. "In 1921, the first ferry ran from the mainland to Misty Island. It ran only once a week back then. Things went fine until one day the fog came in even thicker than this. You couldn't see your hand in front of your face."

"How would you know that?" Aunt Win scoffed. "You were just a baby then."

"This is the story that my father told me. And I'm telling it to you exactly as he told it to me," Jack said firmly.

"I saw a picture of a ghost ferry in the museum today," Dee put in. "Is it the same one?"

"The exact same," said Jack.

"What's the story?" Mr. Forest asked.

Jack settled comfortably back in his chair. "The captain wanted to shut it down, but the ferry owner was a greedy fellow and he insisted that the ferry make its run, despite the foul weather. It was the end of June, and folks then were starting to come over for the summer months. He had a full load of passengers booked to travel both ways. Didn't want to give up the fares, you see."

Jack leaned forward again and looked each of them in the eye, one by one.

"Have you ever been out on the water in a really thick fog? I have. It's the closest thing I can imagine to what it must be like to be dead. There's just gray all around you. No up, no down. No shoreline, no ocean, no sky. Nothing but the grayness and a cold, clammy feeling that goes right through to your bones."

Dee shivered and drew her sweater closer.

"The ferry set out for the mainland at four o'clock. As you know, it's just an hour's run, but by five there was no sign of the ferry. And none at six, seven, or eight. By morning the fog had lifted. All the boats on the island went out to look for the ferry. Rescue parties set sail

63

from the mainland, too." Here, Jack paused dramatically.

"And?" Aunt Win prompted him.

"And no one ever found the ferry or any of the passengers again."

"How could that be?" asked Dee's father skeptically. "They must have gone way off course and pulled in at another harbor."

Old Jack shook his head. "They checked all up and down the coast. They even offered a reward in all the papers for any information on the fate of the ferry. But no one heard or saw anything—not for a while, anyway."

"What do you mean?" asked Eva.

"About six months after that, folks in these parts started seeing lights out on the water—saw them in the middle of the night when no vessel should be moving out there. Or they spotted them on foggy nights like this when no seafarer in his right mind would set sail."

"What were the lights?" Dee asked.

"They were the ferry, of course. The ghost ferry! Folks say it comes to claim lost souls. Once you step onto the ghost ferry, there's no getting off. You sail around in the foggy night forever."

Aunt Win smacked Jack on the arm good-naturedly. "You didn't see any lights," she said. "You're just trying to scare us."

"And succeeding." Eva laughed nervously.

"I've been hearing that story for years," said Aunt Win. "It's just a ghost story, and everyone knows ghosts don't exist."

Only Jack kept a straight face. Dee couldn't tell if he was kidding or not. "Don't take my word for it," he said. "These past few nights all sorts of folks have been seeing the lights of the ghost ferry again. More and more people are talking about it."

"Why would the ferry show up now?" Nicky asked.

"Simple," his grandfather answered. "There's a lost soul roaming the island. A lost soul with no place to go. A soul who's so sad that he or she is ready to be lured onto the ghost ferry. That's when it comes."

Dee could feel a knot slowly forming in the pit of her stomach. Louisa! Could the ghost ferry be coming for her?

"That's just plain silliness," Aunt Win scolded Jack. "No one has even died on this island in over a year. There are no ghosts on Misty Island."

The knot tightened. Dee knew that Aunt Win was wrong.

"Maybe it's silliness, and maybe it's not," Jack said. "I'm just telling you what folks say."

Aunt Win got up. "We're all going to be ready for the ghost ferry if we don't get in out of the damp," she said sensibly. "I baked a blackberry pie this afternoon and I think I hear it calling to me."

"Well, this certainly is a good night for a ghost story," said Dee's father, rising to his feet.

"Yes, I don't know how I'm going to fall asleep now," Eva added. Then they both followed Aunt Win and Jack into the house, leaving Dee and Nicky alone on the porch.

"Grandpa's quite a storyteller," he said.

"He sure is," Dee answered absently.

"Don't let him get to you," Nicky said. "Grandpa tells all kinds of wild stories."

Dee looked at him. How could she explain what she was feeling? Everyone thought Jack was putting them on, but Dee knew he wasn't. And if she tried to talk about Louisa, no one would believe her either.

Where was Louisa, Dee wondered. Dee hadn't seen her since the fight in the cemetery. She had to find her and warn her about the ghost ferry. Louisa herself had said there were no other ghosts on Misty Island. The ghost ferry had to be coming for her!

"Feel like going to a movie or something tomorrow?" Nicky asked suddenly. From the way he twisted the bottom of his windbreaker, Dee could tell he was nervous.

Dee should have been thrilled. But she couldn't imagine going out and having fun while Louisa was in such danger. "No, no, I— I'm sorry, I can't," she stammered.

His face fell. "Is tomorrow bad, or would you just rather not—"

"No, I mean, yes, I would, but—" She couldn't think about dating now. "I'm sorry. I don't feel very well. You'll have to excuse me," she said, turning and running back into the inn.

Dee raced up the winding wooden staircase that led to her room, shut the door tightly behind her, and threw herself down on the four-poster bed. She'd made a fool of herself. Nicky would never ask her out again. But that wasn't the most important thing now, anyway. The important thing was finding Louisa and warning her. That is, if it wasn't already too late. Dee didn't even want to think it, but what if Louisa was already stepping onto the ghost ferry at this very moment?

CHAPTER
8

The first sound Dee heard when she awoke the next morning was the blast of the foghorn. She rubbed her eyes and peered out the bedroom window. Everything was gray. She'd never given much thought to why they called this place Misty Island. But now she realized the name suited it well.

She shivered and pulled her oversize T-shirt tightly around her. It was unusually cool and damp for a summer's day. She walked to the window and looked out. Normally she could see clear to the ocean, but today there was nothing to see. Nothing but a blanket of fog.

Dee pulled on jeans and a sweatshirt. As she rummaged for socks in her top drawer, her fingers tangled in a long filigreed chain. She stopped and gazed down at the delicate wings of the silver dove attached to the silver chain. It had belonged to her mother when she was a girl, and Dee treasured it.

She slipped the pendant over her head and opened the closet door. The pink high-tops were sitting there. No, she wouldn't wear those. She'd given them to Louisa, and Louisa would want them back as soon as Dee found her. And she *was* going to find her, no matter how long it took.

She slipped into a pair of blue canvas espadrilles and ran downstairs.

The dining room was noisy with the clatter of dishes as the guests helped themselves to breakfast from the lavish buffet Aunt Win had set out. Dee heard a babble of complaint about the weather. It seemed that all the guests had visited the museum yesterday afternoon, and last night they'd all seen the one movie playing in town. That was about it for the island's bad weather activities.

Dee took a glass of orange juice and a sticky

bun from the sideboard and stepped out onto the porch. She had to think. Where could Louisa have gone? When she'd first awakened from her long sleep, she had headed straight for the inn. She had no other home. But then, Louisa didn't really need a home—or any shelter at all. She wasn't affected by the cold or the damp. She could be anywhere.

Setting her empty glass down on the railing, Dee marched purposefully down the steps. Louisa always seemed the most comfortable at places that had existed during her lifetime. Dee decided to visit all the oldest places on the island. That was someplace to start, anyway.

Dee got her bike from the side of the inn and pedaled down the gravel drive and onto the twisting main road. She pedaled quickly toward town, turning off at the wide sloping street that led to the harbor. Surely the dock had been there in Louisa's time.

When she coasted into the parking lot, Dee saw the white Misty Island ferry sitting in the slip. It had a large open space for cars at the bottom and two levels for passengers. It was easily three times as big as the small ferry that ran twice a week in the winter months. There was a line of cars in front of it, waiting to drive aboard, and a group of passengers without cars out on the dock.

Dee noticed that the ferry was behind schedule. The first one usually left at eight-thirty, and it was already nine. "I can't believe this!" cried a woman, standing next to her car. "I have to be in Boston this afternoon, and I still have a three-hour drive ahead."

"I'm sorry, miss," said a ferry worker in orange coveralls. "We can't go out in this fog. Maybe it will lift in a few hours, but we're not going anywhere until we get the go-ahead from Interstate Navigation."

Two other drivers joined the woman in complaining to the ferry worker. Dee wanted to jump in and tell them to be patient. She wanted to warn them that another ferry had gone out in the heavy fog and had never been heard from again. She decided against it, though. They'd just think she was some oddball island kid who'd heard one too many spooky stories.

Instead, she walked her bike down to the ferry office. It was the original small wooden building that had stood since the turn of the century. The dock itself was even older, though it had been rebuilt more than once since Louisa's time.

Dee passed the line of unhappy vacationers waiting to get on the ferry and continued out to the end of the pier. Clouds of fog misted up from the water and rolled across the pier. She looked behind to make sure no one was near.

"Louisa?" Dee whispered. "Are you there? Can you hear me?"

She listened. The only sound was the bumping of the ferry as it rocked against the rubber pads on the dock and the slosh of water against the wooden pilings. "Please, Louisa. I have to tell you something very important."

Suddenly Dee became aware of a stirring in the air. It was just a feeling—but a strong feeling—that Louisa was near. "Talk to me, please!" she begged. Everything was quiet. "You're in danger, Louisa," Dee went on. "There's a ghost ferry coming to the island. No matter what you do, don't get on it. Please, you don't have to talk to me if you don't want to. Just let me know if you're here."

Dee waited for a sign, but none came. Instead she saw the man in orange coveralls hurrying toward her. "Are you okay, kid?" he asked. "You look sort of upset."

She smiled at the man. "I'm not jumping off or anything. Thanks for asking though."

"You'd better come inside anyway," he said. "If you slipped and fell, nobody would even notice in this fog."

"Thanks," Dee said again and followed him back up the dock. But when he ran ahead to assist another worker who had called to him, Dee slowed her pace. She had to figure out where to search next. She'd been so certain Louisa was right there, but apparently she wasn't.

When she picked up her bike outside the ferry office, Dee saw two old men coming up from behind the building. They'd obviously been fishing and carried their poles and buckets with them. "Hi, Mr. Culver, Mr. Adams," she said. She knew them because they were friends of Aunt Win's.

"Hi, there, young lady," said Mr. Culver. "Some fog, eh?"

"Sure is," Dee replied, eager to be on her way.

"It hasn't been this thick since the year of the ghost ferry," added Mr. Adams.

At the mention of the ghost ferry, Dee stood still. "You're exaggerating as usual," said Mr. Culver. "We have fog this time of year, and it's always thick as pea soup."

Mr. Adams shook his gray head slowly. "No, Amos, you're wrong. It hasn't been this thick in years."

"Your memory is going, you old buzzard," Mr. Culver said, cackling. The two men smiled at Dee and continued on toward the road.

"Excuse me," Dee called, walking her bike up alongside them. "Can you tell me more about the ghost ferry you mentioned just now?"

"It's just some crazy tale. Don't pay it any mind," said Mr. Culver.

"Crazy, is it?" Mr. Adams objected. "My great-aunt Mabel was on that ferry and we never heard from her again."

Dee gasped. "It's really true then?"

"His great-aunt was an old bat and they never heard from her again because she had a fight with his mother," Mr. Culver declared.

"That may be true," Mr. Adams admitted. "But *no one* ever heard from her. That ferry ran into something mysterious out there in the fog. Something mysterious and evil. And, I'm telling you true, that ghost ferry's come back here!"

"Don't start that again," Mr. Culver snapped.

"I saw the lights just last night," Mr. Adams insisted. "So did Amy Pierce, who takes the money at the museum. Doc Hanson saw the lights, too. And he's a doctor."

"So you saw some lights," said Mr. Culver. "They could have been anything."

"There was a Coast Guard warning last night," Mr. Adams argued. "The late ferries didn't even run."

"Do people have any idea why the ghost ferry would be coming back now?" Dee asked, hoping there was some explanation besides Louisa.

"Folks know, all right," said Mr. Adams, nodding confidently. "The ghost ferry only comes to pick up lost souls. There's got to be a spirit on this island that's lost its way. No doubt about it."

"You superstitious old fool," Mr. Culver said, chuckling. "Let's go have some breakfast."

Mr. Adams turned to Dee. "Don't listen to him. Folks all over the island have seen the lights of the ghost ferry. It's back all right. You go see Mrs. Horace. She'll tell you."

Dee looked up, surprised to realize they'd already reached the busy main road. With a quick wave, the two men hurried off for breakfast at the Misty Island Cafe and Clam Bar.

"Mrs. Horace," Dee repeated. Mrs. Horace's Esoteric Book Shop was on a narrow dirt road in the middle of the island. The local people paid little attention to it. But tourists who discovered it seemed fascinated by the little store—and especially its owner.

The kids at school claimed Mrs. Horace was a witch. One boy insisted that his older brother had seen her dancing alone in the road one night when the moon was full.

Dee had never thought much about Mrs. Horace. Aunt Win knew her forever and said she was a harmless fraud. Other people on the island swore she had psychic powers. Dee had only glimpsed her once when she was shopping in the general store. She had just seemed like a slightly odd-looking old lady.

The thought of going to see Mrs. Horace

didn't much appeal to Dee. Still, she thought, maybe the woman really did have the power to contact the spirit world. Maybe she could help her find Louisa.

CHAPTER
9

The wheels of Dee's bike wobbled down the narrow dirt road through the woods. Around the bend Dee saw a chipped white-shingled house. The porch was cluttered with old furniture and a badly faded sign hung overhead. Dee could barely make out the letters . . . MRS. HORACE'S ESOTERIC BOOKS.

Setting her bike down on the dirt around the porch, Dee climbed the rickety steps. A large white cat hissed at her from his place on a dirty white wicker chair.

The door creaked open and small brass bells over the doorway rang musically. Dee looked to the curtained doorway at the back of the store, but no one came out.

She picked up a shiny paperback book. *"The History of Witchcraft Through the Ages,"* Dee read aloud. On the cover of another book was a picture of a branch with small lavender flowers—*Healing With Herbs: An Ancient Art.*

"Can I help you?" came a voice at Dee's ear.

Startled, she dropped the book. Behind her was a slender woman with a deeply wrinkled face and violet eyes. Her dark hair was streaked with gray and fell loosely to her shoulders. She wore a flowing purple tunic over silky black slacks. Dee stooped to pick up the book. "Sorry, you scared me," she said, looking up at the woman. "I didn't hear you come up behind me."

The woman nodded. "I know," she said. She studied Dee expressionlessly. "I sense you are searching for something," she said.

"Wow!" cried Dee. "How did you know that?"

"Mrs. Horace knows many things." Mrs. Horace's strange violet eyes bore into Dee. "This which you seek has led you to my doorstep."

"That's right," said Dee.

"And yet it is something that cannot be found in books."

"I don't think so, either," Dee agreed. "Unless you have a book about the ghost ferry."

Mrs. Horace stepped back two paces. "You too have seen the lights?"

"No, but I know some people who have, and, and . . ." Dee didn't know how to explain. She wasn't sure she wanted to tell this stranger about Louisa.

Mrs. Horace put her hand on Dee's shoulder. "Would you care to consult the spirit world on this matter?"

Dee nodded. With a wave of a well-manicured hand, Mrs. Horace beckoned Dee to follow her behind the curtain.

Together they climbed a set of narrow stairs that led to an unexpectedly neat parlor. Mrs. Horace seated herself at a small round table and indicated that Dee should take the seat across from her. She held out her soft, white hands. "Place your hands in mine," she said. Dee laid her palms down on top of Mrs. Horace's. The woman's hands were cool and dry.

"I feel the spirits of the ghost ferry in this

81

room," she began in a low voice. "They are very close." She closed her eyes and then she threw her head back. "Yes! Yes! The vibrations are very strong. They have a message for you. They want me to tell you something."

Mrs. Horace's eyes snapped open. "Before I give you the message, perhaps you'd like to give me something." And when Dee only stared at her blankly, she said, "You do understand I get paid for my service?"

Dee was surprised. She hadn't been thinking about money. She reached into her back pocket and pulled out some crumpled bills. "I only have seven dollars," she said, smoothing them out on the table.

Mrs. Horace reached for the money. "That will have to do, I suppose."

Just then a loud crash made Dee jump. A thick book had fallen from the shelf. Mrs. Horace seemed startled, too, but she quickly recovered. "The room is alive with spirits," she said knowingly.

She reached out for the money once again, but quickly drew her hand back as if the money was hot. She gave Dee a reproachful look. "Why did you do that?"

"I didn't do anything," Dee said honestly.

Mrs. Horace's eyes darted around the room. "Someone or something just slapped my hand."

"It wasn't me," Dee insisted.

Mrs. Horace eyed her suspiciously. Once again she reached for the money. As she touched it, a large glass vase floated up off the table—and then dropped, shattering on the floor.

Both Dee and Mrs. Horace jumped to their feet. Mrs. Horace began backing away toward the doorway. "The spirits are obviously very, very angry with you," she said, sounding genuinely frightened.

"Angry with *me?*"

"Well, it's not me!" shouted Mrs. Horace. "They never bothered me until *you* got here!"

The bells over Mrs. Horace's door tinkled. "I have customers," she said, hurrying down the stairs. "I want you to leave right now. And take that money with you."

Dee was alone in the room. "Louisa?" she called softly. "I know you're in here. Please talk to me."

A gentle breeze ruffled the gauzy curtains by the open window, but there was no answer.

Dee shivered. If it wasn't Louisa, then who was in the room? She quickly gathered her money and ran down the stairs.

A young, well-tanned couple had come into the store and were browsing. Dee spotted Mrs. Horace fiddling with some books near the entrance. As Dee passed by, she noticed that the woman's hands were shaking. "And don't come back!" Mrs. Horace yelled.

Don't worry about it, thought Dee as she grabbed her bike and jumped on. She pedaled hard until she hit the paved road, then stopped to catch her breath.

What exactly was going on, Dee wondered. Mrs. Horace *had* seemed to know she was searching for something. She'd said the spirits were near and that was obviously true. But whose spirit was it? Back in Mrs. Horace's parlor, Dee had been sure it was Louisa. She'd almost laughed out loud when Mrs. Horace got her hand slapped. But suddenly Dee wasn't sure of anything.

"Where are you, Louisa!" Dee cried out in frustration. Only the mournful sound of the foghorn answered her.

The tall pines behind Dee seemed to whisper

as their needles rustled in the breeze. Again Dee had the feeling that she wasn't alone. Whoever—or whatever—had been in Mrs. Horace's parlor had followed her out. She was sure of it.

Rubbing the goose bumps from her arms, Dee summoned her courage. "Who are you?" she demanded bravely. "What do you want?"

Suddenly there was a loud snap. Dee's heart leapt into her throat as a low branch cracked behind her. She stood there a moment, straddling her bike, waiting for the spirit to appear, but everything remained quiet.

For the rest of the day, Dee couldn't shake the feeling that the presence was trailing her. But because she didn't know what else to do, she kept looking for Louisa.

She went back to the graveyard and to the old Timmins mansion, which was now boarded up. She searched the old church on the far side of the island and even checked the high bluffs. There was no historic site on top of the bluffs, but Dee remembered Louisa telling her how she sometimes used to go there to look at the ocean and think.

Dee stood at the top of the bluff and watched

the waves crashing down on the rocky shore below. Around the bend she could see a rock jetty jutting out to sea. She realized that Fingers Cove was on the other side. She also remembered the small wooden cabin she and Louisa had discovered there. Mrs. Lockwood's son, William, had been living there when they found it early last fall. But he had since gone to live with his mother, and now it was empty.

That would be a perfect place for a ghost to live, Dee thought. Digging her feet into the sandy dirt, she began the difficult descent down the steep bluff. She had to hang on to the scrubby bushes to keep from falling. Even so, she slipped and took the last few feet of the bluff on her bottom. But finally she was standing on the rocky beach.

Though it had been rough getting down, Dee knew it would be easier to walk along the shoreline to Fingers Cove than it would have been to bike there. The path into the cove was pitted with ditches and sprinkled with big rocks. She'd worry about getting back up the bluff later.

Dee stepped over driftwood and the remains of several damped-out campfires. Because of the weather, there were no swimmers or sunbathers in sight. Even in good weather not everyone wanted to hazard the descent down the bluff— or, for that matter, the difficult climb back up. The sea was rougher here and the shore much rockier than at the other beaches, so it was never exactly crowded. Today it seemed absolutely desolate.

A cold, wet drop plopped down on Dee's forehead. Another hit her cheek. The feeling of being followed persisted. "Who's there?" Dee cried. But again there was no response.

Dee stopped and covered her eyes with her hands. Maybe she was really losing her mind. There was no one there. She was talking to herself like a crazy person.

She sat down on a rock. What if her mother's death had really unhinged her? What if Louisa didn't even exist? Maybe she imagined the whole thing. A shiver ran up Dee's spine. What if this whole winter she'd been hanging out with a figment of her own imagination?

Dee shook off that thought. Louisa might be a ghost, but she was real enough. And now she might be in terrible trouble. Dee *had* to find her.

She continued along the shoreline, jumping from rock to rock. The seawater splashed up and ran under her feet. That and the rain, which was falling harder and harder, made the rocks extremely slippery. More than once, she almost lost her footing.

Finally she turned another bend in the shoreline and came to Fingers Cove. Here the rocks gave way to a bed of soft sand, rimmed by a dense pine forest. The rain was falling steadily now. It was hard for Dee to gauge the time because of the fog, but she guessed it was almost seven in the evening. She'd spent hours searching for Louisa.

Dee realized she'd be in trouble when she got back to the inn. She had forgotten about helping with the breakfast dishes, and she hadn't told anyone where she was going. She would just check this one last spot, she told herself, then she'd head back and face the music.

The beach was deserted and no one was out on the rocky jetties, the fingerlike protrusions that gave the place its name. "Louisa?" she called. Nothing. But as Dee turned toward the forest where the cabin was, she caught sight of something in the water.

Hovering at the end of the jetty, Dee could just make out the murky form of a squarish boat. Its outline wavered in the mist. The boat rose and fell, buffeted by the waves that lapped against the jetty.

Dee peered through the fog. The boat was old. She'd never seen one like it down at the harbor or the marina. And there was no reason for a boat to be anchored over here. It didn't make sense. Unless . . .

"The ghost ferry!" Dee gasped.

CHAPTER

10

Dee's heart raced. Could this really be the ghost ferry? She tried to remember the photo she'd seen in the museum. The picture hadn't been very well focused. It was hard to tell.

She moved down to the shoreline. The boat wasn't nearly as big as the winter ferry. It was only the size of a small cabin cruiser. But of course there hadn't been as many people on Misty Island back then. The ferry *would* have been much smaller.

If this was the ghost ferry, it was awfully near to shore. Too near. Dee was torn between the urge to run back home and her need to know if Louisa was already aboard.

Her loyalty to Louisa won out. Without another thought, she moved out onto the jetty and picked her way over the rocks. She barely dared to breathe. The boat seemed to hang there in the mist. Quiet. Waiting.

Dee forced her legs to carry her closer and closer. She had to know what secrets it held— no matter how frightening they might be. As she walked farther out onto the jetty, the mist around her thickened. She looked down and realized she could hardly see the rocks beneath her feet.

She was almost at the end of the jetty. With her heart crashing against her chest, Dee came up alongside the boat. Close up, she noticed that the boat's paint was blistered and peeling. When she was near enough, she reached out and touched the hull. It was solid enough.

She felt the presence with her very strongly now. Was it a lost soul from the ghost ferry?

Dee told herself not to be afraid. Even if this was the ghost ferry, *she* wasn't a lost soul. It couldn't hurt her. She hoped.

Dee was overcome with curiosity now. Inhaling deeply to steady her nerves, she jumped down off the rocks and onto the deck. The smell of gasoline and fish was strong. Nothing ghostly about that.

She looked around and saw all the normal things you'd see on any boat: a spare tank of gasoline, a compass, an oar, fishing rods, life preservers. There was even a six-pack of beer near the steering wheel.

Dee pulled aside an old tarp in the corner of the boat. Her hand flew to her mouth in fright.

There were two rifles lying there beside each other!

Stay calm, she told herself. *These aren't ghosts, just hunters.* But Dee knew there was no hunting allowed on Misty Island.

Suddenly Dee heard two men approaching. From the sound of their voices, she could tell they were very close. She threw the tarp back over the guns. Panicked, she pulled open the door to the lower cabin and slipped inside. It smelled of sweat and beer. She held her breath, hoping the men were just getting something from their boat and would leave again.

Dee's eyes took in the small cabin. There were two cushioned bunks with pillows on them. She guessed they served as beds. There was also a table, two chairs, and a mirror. That was it. If someone came into the cabin she'd have nowhere to hide.

The men's voices were now very loud. Dee could hear them speak quite clearly. "I'm glad you scoped out that shack," one of them said in a deep, gravelly voice. "If I had to spend another day sleeping on this boat, I'd be crippled for life."

Day? Dee wondered why two men with a boat would be sleeping during the day. But that was good news for her. At least they wouldn't be coming into the cabin to sleep.

"That shack is great," agreed the other, younger-sounding man. "I don't know where else we could have put all those lobsters. They sure looked weird crawling all over one another in that old-fashioned bathtub."

"Yeah," said the first voice. "This island is a gold mine. I've never seen so many lobsters in one place. They practically beg you to haul them out of the water!"

Dee was confused. According to old Jack Dodge, the lobster crop had never been poorer.

"It's a pain getting them in the dark, though,

isn't it, Carl?" said the younger man. "Especially in all this fog. I'm always scared the lights are going to give us away."

The man called Carl chuckled. "Don't you worry about a thing, Lenny. I revived that ghost ferry rumor, but good. Every old geezer on this island is talking about it."

What was going on? Dee wondered. Why would these men want to fool people into thinking the ghost ferry was here?

Lenny let out a low snorting laugh. Dee heard a pop-top snap open.

"Yeah. When I walked into that rinky-dink museum to get out of the rain and saw that picture, I knew we had it made," Carl continued, sounding very pleased with himself.

"Then you started talking it up around town, saying you'd actually seen the ferry," added Lenny. "The beauty part is that now the people who see the lights think they're seeing ghosts— or at least they wonder about it. And the ones who don't see the lights think the ones who do are batty. Genius, pure genius."

Suddenly Dee put the pieces together. So that's what this was all about! These men were stealing lobsters from the local traps! They'd revived the story of the ghost ferry in order to explain their lights flickering at night.

"It's easy to stir up an old legend, especially on a small island like this," said Carl. "No one will ever suspect what this boat is really doing."

She knew that lots of families on Misty Island depended on selling those lobsters for their livelihood. There were laws protecting them from poachers, but the Coast Guard had to catch the poachers first.

Dee knew she had to go tell Officer Munroe what was going on. This explained everything.

And Louisa wasn't in danger! There was no need to worry about her anymore. But now *Dee* was the one in trouble. She had to get off this boat without being seen. These men wouldn't be too friendly if they found her snooping around.

"It's still almost two hours till dark," Lenny was saying. "What do you think?"

"In this fog and rain it won't make a difference," Carl replied. "Nobody can see anything."

"But we won't be able to see either," Lenny pointed out.

"Come on, we've been doing this for five

nights. We know exactly where all the traps are. Let's go," said Carl.

The next sound Dee heard made her gasp. It was the sound of the boat's engine starting up. Dee fought down panic. She didn't want to go out to sea with these creeps. They'd be sure to find her and there would be no place to run. But the men were right outside the cabin door. If they saw her now, she wouldn't have a chance.

Shaking with fright, Dee slid down along the door of the cabin. She felt sick to her stomach. Why wasn't Louisa there with her? They'd been in scary spots before, but always together.

Dee huddled on the floor as the boat chugged out to sea. She completely lost track of the time, but after a long while she could see the dull light fading through the crack at the bottom of the door.

The boat slowed its motors at several spots. Dee heard the sound of lobster traps being hauled in and lobsters being thrown onto the deck of the boat.

"This is ridiculous," Lenny grumbled at the tenth stop. "I can't see a thing. I'm getting the kerosene lamp from inside the cabin."

Dee jumped up as the cabin door was pushed open, squeezing herself into a corner behind it. She clasped her hand over her mouth and nose to keep the sound of her breath from giving her away.

Lenny's flashlight swept the cabin. He entered and began rummaging under one of the beds. "Where is that stupid thing?" she heard him mutter.

Find it. Find it and go, she prayed, pressing herself against the wall. She peeked through the crack between the open door and the wall and saw Lenny squatting on the floor. A beam of light shone just inches from Dee's feet and then moved on.

"Here it is!" he cried, pulling the lantern from under the table.

Dee's shoulders sagged with relief. In another second he'd be gone. Carefully she settled her weight against the wall.

Suddenly Dee was blinded by a bright light shining into her eyes!

CHAPTER

11

A cold streak of pure terror ran along Dee's spine. Lenny's small eyes were dark with fury as he stared down at her. *He must be at least six foot six*, Dee thought. "What are you doing here?" he demanded, grabbing her by the shoulders.

Dee was speechless. The man shook her roughly. His tight grip brought tears to her eyes. "Talk to me, you little brat!"

"Let me go!" Dee cried, squirming violently, trying to break free.

He shoved her out into the middle of the boat, and her head hit the deck with a thud.

"I'm not fooling around, kid. I want some answers," he yelled.

"I—I—I." Dee's head ached. She was too frightened to think straight.

The man named Carl shined his flashlight down on her. He was short and broad with a stubbly beard and red-rimmed blue eyes. "Well, well," he said with a nasty smile. "We seem to have a small problem here."

"She heard everything we said," Lenny pointed out.

"I didn't!" Dee insisted desperately. "I didn't. I—I fell asleep in there. I couldn't hear you talking at all. Not a single word."

The two men exchanged glances. "I believe you, kid," snarled Carl. "But it's not what you heard, it's what you saw—us!"

Dee looked up at him helplessly. "I won't tell anyone about you. Really. I don't care what you're doing. It's none of my business," she lied.

"It's our business to make sure you don't talk," Lenny snarled, yanking her to her feet. "I'm not going to jail because some punk kid got nosy."

Carl grabbed both her wrists in one beefy

hand. "Sorry to have to do this, girlie," he said, and she saw him curl his other hand into a fist. Dee cringed, waiting for the blow to land.

But something stopped him. "*Ooooouuuwww-whhh!*" he cried out, loosening his grip abruptly. "Something bit me!" he growled.

Dee seized the opportunity and pulled away. But a sharp click behind her stopped her in her tracks. "I wouldn't try any funny business," Lenny said, staring down the end of the rifle he was pointing right at her. "Nobody's going to hear a shot fired this far out." He looked over at Carl, who was rubbing his arm. "Want me to?" he asked.

Carl looked from Lenny to Dee and back again. "It's your call," he began. "You—"

"NO!" Dee screamed. Without waiting for the rest of the sentence, she closed her eyes, took a deep breath, and jumped overboard.

Dee heard a single shot fired over her head, and then the icy water hit her like a hammer blow. Down she went, into the pitch-black sea. There wasn't a trace of light anywhere. As she came to the surface, she heard the sound of another gunshot. Terrified, she swam back down, her lungs aching for air.

She swam faster than she ever had in her life. But in the blackness, she had no idea which way she was going. She could be swimming right back toward the boat, for all she knew.

When she could no longer stand it, she came to the surface for a breath. Gasping, she looked around and saw that the boat was only about fifteen yards away. Lenny and Carl were shining their flashlights into the water, but she knew they had lost sight of her.

She'd escaped. Or had she? She was a strong swimmer, but it was raining hard and the sea was cold and choppy. She turned in a slow circle, treading water. She thought she'd let the foghorn guide her, but it was difficult to tell which direction it was coming from. As her eyes got used to the dark, she saw a blurry patch of light far off in the distance. It was probably the lighthouse. She would swim toward it. It might not be the most direct route to shore, but at least she wouldn't be heading out to sea.

She began to swim. A wave caught her unaware and she swallowed a mouthful of salt water. Sputtering, she fought down panic. She raised her head and continued on.

Dee realized her shoes were weighing her down and kicked them off. She pulled off her heavy sweatshirt as well, but decided to keep her jeans and T-shirt.

As she swam, she began to feel hopeful. She was charged with energy and it seemed that she would reach the lighthouse before long. She pictured herself coming up on the shore. Aunt Win would be standing there with a warm blanket and a thermos of hot cider. They'd alert the Coast Guard who would go pick up those two creeps. Dee saw herself bravely laughing in the poachers' faces while they stood handcuffed. She felt sure that everything was going to be okay.

It didn't take long for the hopeful feeling to fade as wave after wave washed over her. She gulped more and more water, her limbs began to feel numb with fatigue, and the cold was making her teeth chatter uncontrollably.

Dee knew she couldn't give up, but she was beginning to lose the strength and the will to go on. The beacon from the lighthouse seemed to move farther away with each passing moment. Though it felt as if she were covering great distances, the light never seemed to get any closer. She began to cry.

The Rime of the Ancient Mariner popped into her head. She tried to concentrate on reciting it to herself in order to forget her fear. It was better, too, not to focus on every stroke her weary arms made. *Water, water everywhere*, she thought to herself. But when she reached that line, she forgot about the rest of the poem. *Water, water everywhere*. The rain, the ocean, her tears.

Water, water, everywhere. The line kept repeating in her head. She knew she was becoming hysterical, delirious. A giant wave thundered over her. She fought her way back up.

She knew she was drowning.

A second wave slapped her in the face. She couldn't catch her breath. A third wave hit her. *Water, water, everywhere*.

Suddenly Dee was strangely happy, almost giddy, as she felt herself sink under the waves. She wouldn't have to swim anymore. It was going to be over very soon. Very soon. *Water, water, everywhere. Then what would happen?* she wondered.

Louisa, she called in her head. *Louisa, will you be there? Maybe we'll be ghosts together. Then we can do things again like we used to. Louisa, why did you go away? Why did you go?*

Then another wave hit Dee and everything went black . . .

Dee had thought the black night was as dark as anything could be. But she'd been wrong. There was not a pinprick of light in this new darkness.

And there was no cold. Or warmth.

She could no longer hear the lighthouse foghorn. Its light had disappeared.

She had the strange sensation of floating. It was as if an invisible hand were lifting her through the air. She felt as light as the goose-down feathers in Aunt Win's comforters.

And then there *was* a sound. Someone was singing in a high, sweet voice. A lullabye. "Hush, hush, sleep tight. Everything will be all right."

She wanted to call out to the person singing, but she couldn't find her voice. *Mom?* she thought, but she couldn't form the words. *Mom? Mom!*

"Hush, hush, sleep tight," the voice kept singing. Dee stopped wondering. She let herself drift off, soothed by the song.

She no longer had any sense of her own body. She was part of the air, part of the night. And she wasn't afraid anymore. She was floating in an endless sea, without a single care. The sweet voice wrapped itself around her. Then she was engulfed by an even greater darkness, the blackness of complete nothingness . . .

CHAPTER
12

Dee blinked and opened her eyes. A pair of worried blue eyes were staring down at her. It took her a moment to come fully awake and realize who they belonged to.

"You okay?" Nicky Dodge asked.

"What?" Dee said blankly. She looked around and saw that she was sitting under a very large pine tree. The needles on the tree glistened with raindrops, but the ground beneath her was dry.

When she tried to move again, the throbbing in her head reminded her of her late-night swim. She remembered Lenny pushing her overboard and struggling to stay above the waves. And that was all she remembered.

So why was she still alive?

"Where am I?" she asked, rubbing her forehead.

"Hutchins Island. You know, the deserted island off the south side," Nicky answered. "Everybody's been looking all over for you. Grandpa and I decided to try the water, just in case you got caught out on a rock after the tide came in or something like that."

Dee saw Jack Dodge about ten yards down the shore, tying his small skiff to a tree that grew near the water. She looked up and realized it was early morning. The fog had lifted and the sun was a bright orange ball hanging low in the sky. A warm breeze licked her cheeks.

"Where's your friend?" asked Nicky.

"What friend?" Dee replied, puzzled.

"The one who waved us down," Nicky said. "Grandpa and I saw a girl. It looked like she had on a long white dress. She was waving to us from the island. That's how we found you."

"Did she have dark red curly hair?" Dee asked excitedly.

"Couldn't see her that well. She might have. As soon as we waved back to her, she stepped out of sight."

Louisa! thought Dee. It *was* Louisa. She was sure of it. Louisa had saved her life! Louisa had snatched her up from the waves and carried her to shore. It must have been Louisa!

"I don't have a friend with me," said Dee.

Nicky looked puzzled. "Then why did you ask if she had red hair?"

"Oh," said Dee. "I was thinking it might be someone I know who sometimes comes to this island. But it probably wasn't."

Dee suddenly noticed that she was wrapped in a large red plaid blanket. She ran her hand across the wool fringe at the end. She'd seen this blanket before. Yes, she'd seen it at the old shack in the woods at Fingers Cove. Louisa must have gotten it for her.

"How's our girl?" asked Jack, joining them. He lifted Dee's chin gently and studied her face. "That's quite a bump you took on your noggin, but your eyes aren't glassy. It doesn't look like a concussion to me. How does it feel?"

"It hurts," Dee answered.

"I'll bet it does," said Jack kindly.

108

"She says there wasn't any other girl on the island with her," Nicky told his grandfather.

"Nobody lives on this island. Are you sure there was no girl?" asked Jack. "You didn't come here with someone else?"

"I'm sure," said Dee.

Jack shook his head in dismay. "You saw her, too, didn't you, Nicky?" The boy nodded. "That beats all. The early sun can throw some funny reflections off the trees out here. She looked mighty real, though."

Dee didn't say anything else, hoping they would drop the subject. Jack held out a strong hand and helped her up. "Come on, then, little lady. If you say there's nobody else here, I guess there isn't. Now let's get you home."

Dee's head cleared a little as she got to her feet. "I'm not sure how I wound up on this island," she said, "but I do know I almost drowned last night. I was picked up on a boat by lobster poachers. They almost killed me just to keep me quiet. We have to call the Coast Guard and alert them. That's why the lobster catch has been so poor this year."

She saw Nicky and Jack exchange glances. She figured they were wondering if the blow to her head had affected her senses. "It really happened. Their boat was docked just across the way at Fingers Cove."

Dee stepped forward to point to the cove. But her legs wobbled and she fell against Nicky. "Here, put your arm around me," he said, leaning toward her.

Dee held him around the waist. She would have felt awkward being so close to him if she hadn't felt so weak. "I know this all sounds crazy, but I'm telling the truth," she said. "I jumped overboard to get away from them. I almost drowned. That's why I'm not sure how I got here."

"Must have washed up on shore," said Jack. "Don't worry. We believe you. *Somebody* sure gave you that knot on your head. We'll go talk to Constable Munroe once everyone knows you're safe. He can contact the Coast Guard."

With Nicky still supporting her, they slowly made their way toward the flat skiff. As soon as they were all in the boat, Jack pulled the chord of the outboard motor, and then they were off.

Smoky clouds of morning mist drifted across the water, but the sky above was blue and the sun was bright. Dee could tell it was going to be a beautiful day.

And she was alive to see it!

Last night she'd almost died. But she was alive now. The sun, the smell of the ocean, the breeze whipping her hair back as they skipped over the small waves—it all seemed so wonderful to her. She couldn't believe she'd ever taken it for granted.

Dee looked at Nicky sitting across from her. His eyes appeared as blue as the sky as he stared out to sea. He was already tan, and she noticed the way his shirt sleeve flapped against the muscles of his upper arm.

Even old Jack was a welcome sight. She gazed at his deeply lined, weathered face and was reminded of the photos in the museum. She'd never looked at him so closely before. She could tell he'd been quite handsome in his younger days. He'd probably looked a lot like Nicky. Now he was old, yet he still was full of energy.

Suddenly Dee realized what Louisa had been talking about in the graveyard the other day. It *was* good to be alive. The sounds, the smells, the sights, the feelings you had for the people you loved—they were all there to be enjoyed.

Louisa was right. Dee *had* been blocking out life. Sure, they'd had great times, exciting times. But she'd been living in a little world, closed off, separate. Dee smiled to herself. It was funny to think that it had taken a ghost to teach her how to live.

Dee wanted desperately to talk to Louisa now. There was so much she had to tell her.

"Well, here we are—safe and sound," Jack interrupted her thoughts as the skiff pulled in at the harbor. "The first thing we do is call your dad and Aunt Win," he told Dee after tying the boat line to the dock. "They must be just about out of their minds."

Nicky helped her out of the small boat. "You were really lucky," he said. "I wouldn't think anyone could survive what you've been through. You must have a guardian angel watching over you."

"I guess I do," Dee answered softly.

Not five minutes later, Aunt Win's Jeep came squealing down the road to the boat landing. Dee's father leapt out before Win even cut the motor.

"Are you all right, baby?" he asked, wrapping his arms around Dee. She noticed there were tears in his eyes. "I thought we'd lost you," he said, hugging her tight. "I couldn't have stood that, not you, too. What happened?"

"I'm okay now, Daddy," Dee said with a small smile. Just then Aunt Win and Eva came running up to join them. "What hurts, sweetie?" Aunt Win asked, touching Dee's forehead tenderly.

"My head, my stomach, my muscles." Dee felt her eyes fill with tears. She had almost forgotten how awful she felt. But now she was really home. She'd survived.

"There, there," her aunt crooned. "Everything is all right." There were dark shadows under Aunt Win's eyes. Dee saw how tired everyone looked. She was sure they hadn't slept a wink all night.

In the next moment Constable Munroe's patrol car pulled into the parking lot. He hurried toward Dee. "What's this about poachers?" he asked.

Dee began to tell her story, but Aunt Win stopped her. "Come back to the inn after she's rested," she told Munroe. "She can tell you everything then." And putting her arm around Dee's shoulder, she ushered her to the Jeep. Mr. Forest stayed behind for a moment, talking to Jack and the constable.

"I'm sorry I didn't tell you where I—" Dee began to apologize.

"That's okay, honey," said Aunt Win. "Save your strength. You're pale as a ghost except for that black and blue lump on your forehead. I don't want to hear another word until you've rested."

Dee nodded. As she climbed into the Jeep, she felt it again—the presence. "Please, Louisa," she sighed. "Don't stay away any longer."

CHAPTER

13

The first thing Aunt Win did when Dee got back to the inn was to fill her with hot chicken soup and wrap her in a fluffy down comforter. Only then did she allow Constable Munroe to ask his questions.

Dee's father's face went pale when he heard how the men had knocked her down and tried to kill her. "I'll go with you," he volunteered when Munroe finished questioning Dee.

"You'd better stay with your daughter, Mr. Forest," the constable advised. "I don't want to be responsible for what you'd do to those guys when we get our hands on them."

"You're right about that," Mr. Forest agreed. And as soon as Munroe left, he helped Dee up to her room and tucked her into bed. Dee could barely keep her eyes open. "Dr. Hanson is away, but his nurse says he'll be back on the noon ferry. Try to rest until he gets here," her father said.

"Dad," Dee began in a weak voice. "Have I been acting strange since Mom died?"

Her father pushed Dee's hair back off her forehead. "Not strange exactly, but you've kept to yourself a lot. You haven't been the sociable girl I once knew. But that's understandable. I haven't been entirely myself either."

"You like Eva a lot, don't you?" Dee said, her eyes starting to flutter.

Mr. Forest hesitated a moment before he answered. "Yes, I do. But it's so soon after your mother's death. I don't know."

"I hope you let yourself love her, Dad," said Dee. "Mom wouldn't mind. She always wanted us to be happy." And with that, Dee fell into a deep, dream-filled sleep.

She dreamt about the lobster poachers. She saw Carl's monstrous face as he was about to strike her, and Lenny looking down the barrel of the gun. Then she dreamt of waves, but in her dream they were tidal waves, sweeping her over the entire earth. The next thing she knew, she was flying. And so was Louisa—right beside her. They were both so happy as they soared high above the clouds . . .

When Dee opened her eyes again, the sun was already setting. Its golden rays splashed through her bedroom window. And at the edge of the bed, gazing out at the sunset, sat a figure dressed in a white petticoat with blue satin ribbons. The light tinged the edges of her auburn hair with a fiery glow.

"Louisa!" Dee cried out joyfully.

Louisa turned and looked at Dee. "How do you feel?" she asked.

"Not great," Dee answered. She tried to sit up but felt too weak. "Thank you, Louisa. You saved my life."

"You got into trouble trying to save me," said Louisa.

"I thought that old lobster boat was the ghost ferry, coming to get you." Dee laughed hoarsely.

"I know you did, and I should have told you not to worry. I was determined not to come back into your life, though. It hurt so much to leave once, I couldn't bear to come back and then have to leave again. It was stupid of me. I blame myself for everything that happened to you."

"How did you know what was going on?" Dee asked.

"I stayed with you. I wanted to make sure you were all right."

This time Dee did manage to sit up. "It *was* you, then. You were with me all the time. I knew someone was following me. You slapped Mrs. Horace's hand, didn't you?"

Louisa's face lit up with a smile. "That old bat! She wasn't in touch with any spirits. She was just after your money. I couldn't let her take it."

"But she did know I had come there looking for something," Dee pointed out.

Louisa shook her head. "People in your time think they're so sensible, but honestly, Dee, sometimes you could use a little old-fashioned sense. If a young girl comes to a store like that all by herself, she must be searching for *something*. It's obvious. She simply took her clues from what you said."

"You're right. I feel really dumb," said Dee. "But I didn't know what else to do." Dee's eyes lit up. "You bit Carl, too. I know you did."

Louisa looked embarrassed. "That was horribly savage of me, I know."

"Savage!" cried Dee. "He was about to hit me so hard I'd never have gotten up again! He's the savage one, not you. But why didn't you let me know you were there? I was scared out of my wits."

"I'm sorry. I was just being stupid. I had it in my head that if you could get out of this without me, you would realize you don't need me. I thought I was being noble."

"What happened in the water?" Dee asked.

"I stayed with you until you started to go under. You're such a good swimmer, I thought you could make it. When I realized you were in trouble, I lifted you up."

"I heard singing," said Dee.

"That was me," said Louisa. "Whenever I'm terribly frightened, I sing the lullaby my mother used to sing to me. It makes me feel a little braver."

"Why were you frightened?"

"I didn't know if we'd make it to shore. Flying is very difficult for me, and flying with you was even harder. I was afraid I might drop you. Besides, you had passed out. I didn't know if I'd waited too long. Thank goodness that little island was there. I set you down under that tree. Then I went back to the cabin we discovered because I remembered seeing blankets there. I wanted to bring you there, too, but my arms were giving out."

"I didn't know ghosts got tired," said Dee.

"I don't think they do. But something strange has been happening to me lately. I haven't been feeling quite myself all summer. Anyway, I collapsed right next to you once I came back with the blanket." She laid a gentle hand on Dee's foot. "You're all right now. And that's the only thing that matters."

Louisa got up and headed toward the window. She looked back at Dee and smiled sadly. Dee sensed that her friend was leaving again. "Wait!" she said. "Don't go. I've realized some things since we talked the other day."

Louisa turned back, interested.

"You were right about me hiding from life. I see that now. But can't we make a deal? If I go out and do things with other people, couldn't you still stay around?"

"Do you promise?" Louisa asked doubtfully. "You'd have to make some new friends. Otherwise, I'd start feeling guilty again, and that wouldn't do either of us any good at all."

"I promise," said Dee. "I'll force myself to be the most sociable girl on Misty Island. How's that?"

"All right," Louisa agreed. "I don't really want to go."

Dee tried to swing her legs off the bed, but a wave of fatigue pushed her back down onto her pillow. "What *do* you want, Louisa?" she asked. "What would be the best thing for you?"

Louisa stretched across the end of the bed. "I want to join my family," she said sadly. "I don't belong in the land of the living anymore. If you weren't here, it would be unbearable." She looked at Dee seriously. "I'd be so lonely that if a real ghost ferry did show up, I might just walk onto it. And you won't always be here, Dee."

"Yes, I will."

"No. You'll either go back to Cambridge, or you'll grow older and marry and have children.

One way or another, you have to move on. I have to move on, too." Tears welled up in her eyes. "You can't imagine what it's like—not belonging in this world, not being able to find my way into the next one."

"Please don't cry, Louisa," said Dee. "We're so close now. You only need to help one more relative and then you can join your family. We'll find someone. I know we will!"

CHAPTER
14

Dee woke up the next morning feeling much better. Dr. Hanson came by right after breakfast. He examined her carefully and announced that as far as he could see, she'd come through her ordeal in one piece. "You're a mighty lucky girl," he said. "It's unbelievable, but I'd say you were just fine."

Constable Munroe showed up a few hours later to report that the Coast Guard had picked up the two poachers. The two thieves had returned to Fingers Cove confident Dee hadn't survived her plunge into the ocean. It turned out that they were wanted up and down the

New England coast for poaching. "We think they're working for a bigger outfit," the policeman explained, "an outfit that's trying to put the little guys out of business and monopolize the lobster industry. I'm putting you in for a special citizen's award, Dee. We never would have caught them without you."

"It was all kind of by accident, but I'll take the award anyway," Dee said with a laugh.

After he left, Dee walked down to the front yard and found Louisa there. "I'm going to ride over to the bay now and see if I can find those kids who were sailing the other day," she told Louisa. "Will that make you happy?"

"A wonderful idea," Louisa said approvingly.

"What will you do?" asked Dee, worried that Louisa would be lonely.

"I am going to go up to your room, lie down on your bed and read your copy of *Around the World in Eighty Days*. I've never spent a whole day simply being lazy. It sounds wonderful to me."

"Me, too," Dee agreed. "I think I'll get a book, too, and—" At Louisa's warning look, she stopped in midsentence. "Never mind. I'll go down to the bay and see who's around."

"I'll still be here when you get back," Louisa said. "Unless I've decided to go around the world in eighty days," she added mischievously. "And in that case I'll leave a note."

Dee went back and put her bathing suit on under her shorts and shirt. After assuring Aunt Win, Eva, and her father that she felt fine, she got on her bike and rode down the gravel path and out onto the road. She passed through town and was waiting at the stop sign near the museum when Mrs. Lockwood's son, William, pulled up in a pickup truck beside her. "Hi, there," he called out the window.

Dee smiled at him. Louisa and she had helped reunite Mrs. Lockwood and William after a long separation. That had been their first success in the relative-finding project. "My mom says you're coming over sometime to look at her old pictures in the attic," William said.

"I'd like to," Dee answered. And suddenly she lost interest in going to the bay. She knew she'd promised, but she could still go later that afternoon. "Are you heading home by any chance?" she asked.

"Sure am. Want to come over and look at those things now?" William asked.

"Yes, I do. Thanks," said Dee. William hopped out of the truck and put her bike in the back of the pickup. She climbed up into the cab beside him.

Before long they were turning up a narrow drive toward an old, three-story Colonial-style house. Several wings had been added on to the original building, giving it a rather rambling appearance.

The last time Dee had visited Mrs. Lockwood, the willow in the front yard had been bare and spindly. Now it was in full bloom, its graceful branches waving gently in the breeze. William pulled the truck into the driveway, and then Dee followed him along the front path and into the house.

"Mom, I brought a visitor," William called as they stepped into the cool, dark hallway.

Mrs. Lockwood appeared in the hallway. She was holding a potted orchid in her hands. "What was that, William? I was out in the greenhouse and couldn't quite hear—" She smiled when she saw Dee. "What a nice surprise!"

"Hi, Mrs. Lockwood," said Dee. "I came to look at your old photos, if that's still all right."

126

"Yes, of course it is. I see that museum show aroused your interest. Come right along." She led Dee down a narrow back hallway and opened a door. "You'll forgive me if I don't come up with you," Mrs. Lockwood apologized. "My orchids need me right now. I always water them at one o'clock sharp!"

"That's okay," said Dee, glad she'd get to look through the albums by herself. "I know where everything is."

Dee climbed the steps to the attic landing. She remembered it from the time she'd been up there with Louisa several months before. That visit had been interrupted by Mrs. Lockwood's other son, Harry, who'd been trying to steal a valuable coin collection from his own mother. But now, Dee thought, she'd have all the time she needed to examine the albums carefully.

The attic was one long room divided by tall screens and piles of cartons. Old drop cloths covered several bulky pieces of furniture. All the things that fall into disuse in the course of a lifetime were leaning haphazardly against the walls: fishing poles, a guitar with a broken string, empty fish tanks, stacks of magazines.

The windows on either side of the attic were

extremely dirty. Broken, yellowed shades hung halfway down. The little bit of sunlight that made its way into the dark room was filtered to a gentle amber.

Dee headed straight to the center of the attic. She knelt down there and blew the top layer of dust off an old steamer trunk. She yanked the lid up, releasing the musty smell of decaying paper and mildew. Digging through piles of old documents, newspapers, and magazines, Dee finally reached the thick black photo album she'd seen once before.

She turned the cracked pages that featured Mrs. Lockwood with her husband and little Harry and William. She kept going backward as the photos went from color to black and white. Then she picked up another, even older album, where the pictures were all sepia brown. Some of these pictures she'd seen before, but she still found them fascinating.

She studied a photo of a man with a full beard and a fisherman's cap. The last time they were in the attic, Louisa had told Dee it was a picture of her father. There were pictures of her mother, her brother, and even Louisa herself.

Dee looked carefully at the picture of Louisa.

Everyone else in the photos looked stiff, almost as if they were afraid of the camera. Only Louisa looked relaxed and happy. Dee knew she was right—Louisa had been a special kind of person, even way back then. She set the picture of Louisa aside. She was going to ask Mrs. Lockwood if she could keep it.

Some of the photos had been neatly captioned by someone with an elegant, sharply slanted handwriting. *"Edward Lockwood, aged eight,"* Dee read beneath the one of Louisa's little brother. Many of the others weren't identified at all.

Mrs. Lockwood had already told her that she had no other family on the island. What Dee needed to do was trace another family line— someone who had married a Lockwood and had a different name, but might still live here.

Dee turned the pages. There were pictures of Misty Island, like the ones she'd seen in the museum. The people and places were all there, but she couldn't put the pieces of the puzzle together. There simply wasn't enough information to lead her to another relative.

She closed the album, frustrated that it had revealed nothing more about Louisa's family.

As she went to place it back inside the trunk, several loose pictures slid out of the album. "Darn," muttered Dee, gathering them up off the floor. She was about to tuck them back inside when the top picture in the pile made her gasp.

It was her own mother—only it wasn't!

The woman in the tinted photo was clearly from another era. She wore her hair swept up in a topknot. A high lace collar covered her long neck. Yet she looked to Dee almost exactly like her own mother. She had the same merry round eyes, the same delicate nose. This woman's jawline was squarer than Dee's mother's, but she had exactly the same lovely, upturned mouth.

Dee stood and took the picture to the window. She needed more light to make sure she was seeing correctly. In the light the resemblance became even more striking. The arch of the woman's eyebrows, the tilt of her head . . . Everything about this woman reminded Dee of her mother.

Dee's hand flew to her mouth in surprise when she noticed the necklace the woman was wearing around her neck. It was a silver dove on a delicate chain, exactly like the one her mother had given her.

In fact, Dee realized, it *was* the one her mother had given her. It had been her mother's before she passed it on to Dee. She'd told Dee that it was one of a kind, hand hammered by a silversmith in Virginia and handed down among the women in her family for generations.

But how could that be? And who was this woman? Dee turned the photo over in her hand. There was an inscription written on the back: *"To Louisa and Edward, from your loving Aunt Rose."* Under that, someone else had printed: Rose Lockwood Meredith, 1895.

Dee's heart skipped a beat. Her mother's maiden name had been Linda Meredith. The resemblance, the pendant, the name—they all added up to one thing. Dee's mother was related by blood to the Lockwood family. This woman was Dee's great-great-grandmother. And she was also Louisa's aunt. That made Dee and Louisa distant cousins!

Dee couldn't believe it. But it had to be true! *She* was Louisa's missing fourth relative.

CHAPTER
15

Dee dashed down the attic steps and found Mrs. Lockwood standing in the hallway with a worried look on her face. "Gracious, dear, what's the matter? I could hear you clattering down those steps all the way from the greenhouse," she said.

"Sorry, Mrs. Lockwood, it's just that I—"

"Something frightened you up there, didn't it?" Mrs. Lockwood cut her off. "Don't worry. I spent one whole winter thinking there were ghosts in the attic. It turned out there were squirrels up there, not ghosts. I grant you it's a bit spooky, but there's nothing to be frightened of."

"I'm not afraid of ghosts," Dee said. "And I'm not frightened now. I'm just so excited." She showed Mrs. Lockwood the picture of Rose Meredith. "I think the woman in this picture is a relative of mine."

Mrs. Lockwood took the photo from her, then put on the pair of glasses she wore around her neck. "Good heavens!" she said, inspecting the picture and looking back at Dee. "There is a strong resemblance between you two. I can see it in the eyes."

"You think so?" asked Dee, pleased. "Everyone says I have my mother's eyes. And this woman looks exactly like my mother." She went on to explain about the pendant and the names. She didn't leave anything out—except of course the part about Louisa.

"Mrs. Lockwood, I know this is a big favor, but could I have this picture?" Then she held out the photo of Louisa. "And this one, too?"

Mrs. Lockwood hesitated. "These are irreplaceable family mementos," she said, as if thinking out loud.

"I would treasure them. You don't know how much," Dee pressed. She had never wanted anything in her life as much as she wanted these pictures. "If you want to give me only one, I'd be happy just to have the one of the girl," she added.

Mrs. Lockwood gazed at the picture of Louisa. "I'm not even sure who this young girl is. What makes you want her picture so badly?"

"I can't explain. There's something about her face," Dee said, trying to be as truthful as possible. "In some strange way, I feel as though I know her—as though I've always known her."

Tapping the photos against her palm, Mrs. Lockwood seemed to be considering Dee's request. "How can I say no to you when you've done so much for my family," she said at last. "Go ahead, dear. Take both pictures."

Impulsively Dee threw her arms around Mrs. Lockwood's neck and kissed her soft cheek. "Thank you so much. You can't imagine what this means to me!"

"I can see it means a lot," said Mrs. Lockwood, looking bewildered but pleased. "Would you like some lunch?"

"If you don't mind, I'd like to get home and show these pictures to someone," Dee said.

"You'll come back another time, then?" said Mrs. Lockwood hopefully.

"Sure, I'd love to," Dee answered, making her way toward the door. "Thank you. Thank you again, Mrs. Lockwood."

With a final wave, she ran out the front door. Then, after carefully slipping the photos into the front pocket of her shirt, she jumped on her bike. Filled with excitement, she rode quickly back to the inn.

Minutes later Dee threw her bike down on the front lawn, bounded up the front steps, and raced up to her bedroom. She stopped short in the doorway, her eyes quickly scanning the empty room. The window was open and the volume of *Around the World in Eighty Days* lay open on her bed, but there was no sign of Louisa. Then, as if a breeze were blowing it, one of the pages turned.

"Louisa! Are you here?" cried Dee. "I have to see you. I have big news."

Slowly Louisa's outline formed on the bed. Then she became solid. "Sorry, I was so involved in the book that I didn't see you," she said. She rolled over lazily on the bed. "I feel sort of funny today. Not bad, exactly, sleepy almost. A nice, dreamy kind of sleepy. Perhaps carrying you over the waves took more out of me than I realized."

"I have news that will wake you up," Dee said, stepping briskly into the room.

Suddenly Aunt Win came up behind her. "There you are," she said excitedly. Dee looked quickly to her bed. Louisa was gone.

"There's a reporter downstairs from the *Misty Island Gazette*. He's been waiting to talk to you," Aunt Win announced. "They want to put your picture on the front page."

"Oh, Aunt Win, I look a mess," Dee protested. She didn't want to go downstairs. She wanted to tell Louisa her news. "Can he wait until I change?"

"You look wonderful just as you are," said Aunt Win. She put her arm around Dee's shoulder and walked her down the hall. "You have roses in your cheeks and your eyes are bright. That's what people will notice."

Dee was about to argue, but Eva met them on the stairs. "Come on down, Dee. You're a heroine. The photographer wants your picture right now so they can print it in the morning paper. Isn't it exciting!"

"Yes, it is," Dee said. She didn't seem to

have an alternative, so she decided to go down and talk to the people and then come back for Louisa.

At the bottom of the stairs, standing with Dee's father, was a young man in shorts and a white T-shirt. Beside him stood a young woman in a madras plaid sundress. She had a camera slung around her neck. Dee had seen them both in town during the winter but had never spoken to them.

"Here's our heroine!" said the woman. "Stand over there with your aunt." Dee stood beside Aunt Win as the woman snapped the picture. Then the photographer posed her between her father and Eva.

"How's this for the headline?" said the reporter. " 'Niece of Prominent Innkeeper Helps Nab Poachers.' "

" 'Risks Life Nabbing Poachers'!" Aunt Win corrected.

"Right, that's even better," the reporter said agreeably.

After several more photos, Dee told her story to the reporter, who got it all on a portable tape recorder. The reporter shook his head in wonder when she came to the part about diving overboard. "Wow! It's a miracle you survived. How does it make you feel to have come through a life-threatening experience like that?"

Dee thought for a second. "It made me realize that someday I am going to die. But until that time comes, I want to enjoy my life as fully as I can."

Her father put his hand on her shoulder tenderly. She smiled up at him.

Just then Nicky Dodge came in the front door. He backed up automatically when he saw all the people in the hallway. "Come in, Nicky. Come in," said Aunt Win. "This is the young man who saved Dee, along with his grandfather," she told the reporter.

"I didn't really . . . I—" Nicky protested modestly.

"I have to get a picture of you two together," said the photographer, moving Dee next to Nicky. Dee felt suddenly shy standing so close to him.

"Look over at Nicky, Dee," the photographer said. "Smile at him. Remember, he saved your life." Dee looked at Nicky and saw that his face was bright red with embarrassment. She smiled genuinely, and he smiled back.

Flash! The picture was taken. "That's the end of the roll," the photographer announced. "I want to go develop these right away."

As the woman spoke, Dee could imagine what the pictures would look like. She'd be standing with her family and friends much the same way the people in the museum photos had posed almost a hundred years ago. It occurred to her that a hundred years from now someone might find the pictures that had just been taken and wonder who the people were and what their lives had been like. Maybe they'd find them in an old trunk, or uncover a yellowed copy of the *Misty Island Gazette*.

"I've cooked up a big batch of spaghetti and red clam sauce for lunch," said Aunt Win. "The clams are Misty Island's finest. You're all invited."

Nicky turned to Dee. "I just came to see if you were all right," he said. "I don't want to interrupt your lunch or anything."

"You're not interrupting," Dee said. "Please stay."

"Okay, if you're sure."

"Sure I'm sure," Dee said.

The group sat down at the dining-room table. Eva and her father set the table and Aunt Win brought out a steaming pot of pasta and a bowl of rich, sweet sauce. The room smelled of fresh basil and tomatoes.

"You folks going to the dance down at the harbor tonight?" asked the reporter, twirling the spaghetti on his fork.

"We're going," said Eva, smiling at Dee's father. "I'm looking forward to it. I hear the band is great. And they'll be steaming clams and lobsters. Good music and good food—that's my idea of a perfect combination."

"I didn't even know there was a dance," said Dee, wiping sauce from the corner of her mouth.

"That's our Dee." Aunt Win laughed. "Always with her head in the clouds."

"No more," said Dee. "I've decided to get into the swing of things from now on."

"Well, good for you!" said Aunt Win as she ladled more sauce onto Dee's plate.

"Want to come down to the dance with us?" asked Eva.

Dee didn't want to tag along with her father

and Eva on a date, but she remembered her promise to Louisa. "Okay," she said. "If you're sure I won't be in the way."

"Are you kidding?" said Eva. "We'll be proud to be seen with the local heroine."

"Win?" said Mr. Forest. "Care to join us?"

"Thank you very much, but I'm already going—with my own date," Aunt Win replied with a wink.

"I wonder who that could be?" Dee's father teased.

At that very moment Jack Dodge appeared at the dining-room entrance. Everyone burst out laughing.

"What's so darned funny?" he asked gruffly.

"Ignore them, Jack," said Aunt Win. "They've gone soft in the head."

Jack had come to invite them all out fishing. Dee was torn. She was bursting to tell Louisa her news. Yet she'd promised to do things with other people. "Just let me run upstairs for a minute," she said as the others began leaving the table.

She took the stairs two at a time and rushed into her room. The window was still open, but the book lay closed on the bed. "Louisa?" she said. "Louisa! Come out. I have to tell you something. It's important."

But this time there was no answer. Louisa wasn't there.

CHAPTER

16

Dee opened her top dresser drawer and fished under her socks for the silver pendant. She draped it across her fingers and admired the workmanship.

Then she pulled the photos from the pocket of her shirt. There was no doubt about it. This was the same pendant that Rose Meredith was wearing in the photo. She wished Louisa would hurry back so she could show it to her.

As Dee put the photos and the pendant back in the drawer, a sheet of paper fluttered to the floor from the top of the dresser. It was a note from Louisa. "Don't worry about me," Dee read. "I have gone for a walk."

Disappointed, Dee crumpled up the note and hurried downstairs to join the others. They all drove down to the harbor where Jack kept his boat docked, Dee and Nicky with Aunt Win in her Jeep, Eva and her father in Jack's old Mustang.

It was a perfectly clear day, and Jack's boat was big and beautiful. They all climbed aboard and sailed out into the ocean. As soon as they hit the open sea, Jack brought fishing poles and bait up from the cabin below.

Dee couldn't quite get her mind off Louisa, but she forced herself to pay attention to what was going on around her. She even reeled in a sea bass.

It was seven by the time they docked the boat. "I guess I'll see you down at the dance tonight," said Nicky, offering Dee his hand as she stepped from the boat to the pier.

"You're going?" she asked.

"If you are," he said.

"Then I'll see you there."

"If it's okay with you," Nicky said as they walked up the dock, "I'll come by for you."

"That would be good," Dee said. "I'm glad you're not mad at me about the other night. It wasn't personal. I had this problem on my mind."

"It's okay," he said with a shrug. "I'll see you around eight-thirty."

When they got home, Dee hurried up to her room again. And again there was no sign of Louisa. Eva rapped on the open bedroom door. She was holding a dress over her arms. "I saw this in town the other day and it seemed so perfect for you that I had to buy it. I was saving it for your birthday next week, but I figured you might want to wear it tonight."

"Thank you," said Dee, touched by Eva's thoughtfulness. She held the dress up in front of the mirror. It was made of a soft lavender cotton. The dress wrapped in the front and flared out into a graceful skirt that fell below her knees. "It's beautiful," Dee said sincerely. "I will wear it tonight."

"It just seemed right for you," said Eva, giving Dee a quick hug before leaving the room.

Dee showered and put on the new dress. It fit her perfectly. Then she slipped into a pair of white sandals. And finally she put the silver pendant around her neck. "Come on, Louisa," she muttered.

Dee drifted over to the window and gazed out. The last light of day was bathing everything in shades of pink, gold, and gray. Suddenly she saw a figure standing at the very edge of the lawn, looking out to sea. It was Louisa.

Grabbing the photos, Dee ran downstairs and out onto the lawn. "Louisa, where have you been?" Dee called as she neared her friend.

"Walking," Louisa answered simply.

Dee wondered why Louisa was standing there in plain sight, but she was too excited about the picture to ask. "Louisa, you'll never guess what I discovered today. It's the most wonderful thing." She showed Louisa the picture of Rose Lockwood Meredith.

"Aunt Rose," Louisa said fondly as she took the picture from Dee. "Where did you get this?"

"Mrs. Lockwood's. Louisa, this may be your aunt—but it's also my great-great-grandmother. Your aunt Rose married my great-great-grandfather. Do you know what that means?" And without waiting for Louisa to reply, she cried, "It means *we're* related!"

Louisa gazed at Dee. Slowly a smile formed on her lips. "So it's you." She laughed softly. "All day long I've sensed that something had changed, that I was almost there. Yet we hadn't found a relative. I didn't understand it. Now I do. I suppose when I picked you out of the ocean that counted as helping you."

Dee touched her hand. "Louisa, that wasn't the first time. You've helped me in a million ways. I would have been the saddest person on earth this winter if it hadn't been for you."

Louisa put her arms around Dee and the two girls hugged each other tightly. Louisa felt very fragile to Dee, but Dee held on tightly.

"I knew *something* was happening," Louisa said. "That's why I wanted to walk. I needed to see everything one last time. I stayed visible so I could look at myself once more before . . ."

"Before what?" asked Dee.

"I'm not sure," said Louisa, glancing away. Her face had never looked more lovely, drenched in the pink light. Her white petticoat dress and her dark red curls fluttered softly in the ocean breeze. "It's like a gentle pull, like the tide. I've been feeling it all day. It keeps getting stronger. And I feel so happy, Dee. So peaceful and unbelievably happy."

Dee's hand went to her mouth. A tear spilled over. "Oh, Louisa. This is it, isn't it?" she cried, her voice catching in her throat. "You're going away. You're going away for good."

Louisa nodded. "Yes, I can feel it. Don't worry about me. I'm going to be fine, better than fine." Dee couldn't tell if it was the glow of the sunset, or something more, but a radiant light illuminated Louisa's face. "I should have known we were related," Louisa said. "I've always felt as if we were sisters."

"So have I," said Dee.

Louisa looked over to the ocean. Her face lit up with a joyous smile. "I see them, Dee," she said excitedly. "My mother and papa and Edward. There they are."

Dee looked, but she didn't see anything.

"I'm coming, Mother, Papa!" Louisa called gently, her voice filled with emotion. She turned back to Dee. "Thank you, Dee. Thank you with all my heart."

"I'm going to miss you so much!" Dee sobbed. "I don't want you to go."

"I have to go. I don't belong here anymore." Louisa squeezed Dee's hand. "I love you," she said. "You're the best friend I've ever had. I'll never forget you."

As she spoke, the silvery light around her grew

brighter and brighter, until it seemed to shine forth from Louisa herself. Louisa looked to the sunset and then back one last time at Dee. Her eyes were soft with love and happiness . . .

And then she was gone.

Dee felt as though her heart would burst, the ache was so strong. She sat on the grass and buried her face in her hands. Hot tears coursed down her cheeks. She'd worked so long for this moment. She hadn't realized it would hurt so much.

After a while her tears subsided. She wiped her eyes and gazed down at the picture of Louisa she held in her hand. She would always remember Louisa as she was in that photo, her eyes alive with sparkling laughter.

"I'll never forget you either, Louisa," Dee whispered. "We'll be friends forever."

Dee sat for a long while, looking out at the ocean. The orange ball dropped below the horizon. For a moment it was reflected brilliantly in the water. And then it was gone.

Dee slowly got up and made her way back to the inn. Aunt Win had turned the lights on. Guests were pouring out of the front door, probably on their way to the dance.

She hung back in the twilight, not wanting anyone to see her tear-stained face. Aunt Win came out onto the porch. Dee couldn't remember ever seeing her in a dress, but tonight she looked so pretty in a simple blue shift. She'd even set her red hair so that it curled up on top. Dee saw Jack come out onto the porch, too. She smiled at the sight of him in an impeccably tailored blue blazer. They looked nice together, she thought.

Next Eva and her father joined them. Eva had bought herself a new white dress. Dee saw her father reach out and take Eva's hand. Eva turned and kissed him lightly on the lips.

"Hi," came a voice behind her.

Dee wiped her eyes quickly. It was Nicky. He looked handsome, too, in a plain white shirt and khaki pants. "You okay?" he asked when he saw her face.

"Uh-huh," Dee said, nodding.

"You look kind of upset. We don't have to go if you don't want to," he said.

"I'll be all right," she assured him. "I was thinking about a friend I miss a lot. But she'd want me to go to the dance. I'm sure of that."

"Okay," he said. "You look really pretty tonight."

"Thank you," said Dee. "Let me go get a sweater and I'll be right back." She ran upstairs and put the pictures of Louisa and Rose Meredith in her top drawer. Then she took Louisa's picture out again and propped it against the mirror. Tomorrow she would buy a frame to put it in.

Dee grabbed a sweater and went back down. Nicky was waiting with the others on the porch. "You look lovely, my dear," said her father.

"So do you," she said, squeezing his hand.

"Shall we go?" asked Aunt Win.

"Feel like walking?" Nicky asked Dee. "It's not that far." Dee agreed, glad to have a little more quiet time before the dance. The others piled into Aunt Win's Jeep and waved goodbye.

As Nicky and Dee set off down the gravel drive, he reached out and took her hand. "Do you mind?" he asked.

"No. I don't mind," she answered.

They walked in silence down to the road. She could hear the ocean washing up on the shore. "Look," said Nicky, pointing to the darkening sky. A flock of birds flew over the ocean. Behind them, one small bird hurried to catch up with the others. "I wonder how he got separated," Nicky said. "I hope he makes it."

"He will," Dee said softly. They stopped and watched the small bird's progress. Soon he was soaring with the others, once again part of the flock. Dee felt her eyes brim with tears.

"Why are you crying?" Nicky asked.

"Because I'm happy," she said, smiling through her tears. "I'm happy that the bird made it back to its family. That's all."

She was glad Nicky didn't laugh or tease her. They continued walking toward town. Dee took a deep breath of the salt air and gazed out over the ocean. She felt very quiet inside, as if a part of her life had ended, and something new was about to begin.

Yet, no matter what her future held, she was sure of one thing. She'd never forget the days she and Louisa had spent together, haunting the shores of Misty Island.

ABOUT THE AUTHOR

EMILY CATES was born in New York City but she spent her summers on the coast of Maine, which gave her the inspiration for the Haunting with Louisa trilogy. She has written several books for adults and has published poetry in several journals. Ms. Cates now divides her time between Boston, Massachusetts, and Block Island, Rhode Island, which is very much like Misty Island in the Haunting with Louisa trilogy.

Magical Skylark 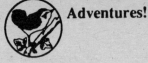 Adventures!

☐ **THE CASTLE IN THE ATTIC**
by Elizabeth Winthrop   15601 $3.50
William is sure there's something magical about the castle he receives
as a present. When he picks up the tiny silver knight, it comes to life!
Suddenly William is off on a fantastic quest to another land and time—
where a fiery dragon and an evil wizard are waiting to do battle...

☐ **THE PICOLINIS**
by Anne Graham Estern   15566 $2.75
Jessica and Peter Blake are thrilled when their parents buy a wonderful
antique dollhouse. But now they hear noises at night...music and voices
that seem to come from the dollhouse. Are the Picolini dolls alive?
The Blake children embark on an exciting and dangerous adventure
in search of lost treasure.

☐ **THE PICOLINIS AND THE HAUNTED HOUSE**
by Anne Graham Estern   15771 $2.95
Jessica and Peter discover a secret passageway in the house across the street
that thieves have been using for years. Now they want to find the thieves!
Can the Picolini dolls help them?

☐ **THE GHOST WORE GRAY**
by Bruce Coville   15610-1 $2.75
Sixth grader Nina Tanleven and her best friend Chris are visiting
an old country inn when suddenly the ghost of a young confederate soldier
appears! They know he's trying to tell them something. But what?

☐ **THE GHOST IN THE THIRD ROW**
by Bruce Coville   15646-2 $2.95
For Nina Tanleven nothing is scarier than trying out for a part in the school
play...except seeing a ghost sitting in the audience! Soon strange things
begin to happen and it's up to Nina to solve the mystery!

From Bantam-Skylark Books
IT'S

From Betsy Haynes, the bestselling author of the Taffy Sinclair books, comes THE FABULOUS FIVE. Follow the adventures of Jana Morgan and the rest of THE FABULOUS FIVE in Wakeman Jr. High.